W9-BYF-796

Copyright © 2019 by Jud Widing

Cover artwork by Heather McMordie
http://www.heathermcmordie.com

Title design by Boy Bison
Instagram: @boybisonzines

All rights reserved. This book or any portion thereof may not be
reproduced or used in any manner whatsoever without the express
written permission of the author except for the use of brief
quotations in a book review.

Designed by Jud Widing
Edited by Gene Christopher

www.judwiding.com
Facebook/Twitter/Instagram: @judwiding

THE LITTLE KING OF CROOKED THINGS

Thank you so much!

Enjoy!!!

BY

JUD WIDING

Thank you so much!

Enjoy!!!

ONE

NEAR THE END of Brobson Lutz's ninth February on Earth, Mom told him that he had been born in sin, which was very confusing because until then she'd always maintained he'd been born in Philadelphia.

Brobson knew what sin was, mostly from Bible Study but sometimes from experience. He'd always been under the impression that sin was a *thing*, though, not a place. You committed a sin, but you couldn't commit a Philadelphia, right? Brobson definitely hadn't. But being a suburban boy with a bicycle and an imagination, he had certainly committed sins.

Heck (sorry), just yesterday he said a swear. He had tried to jump over this huge puddle on the playground, but he came up short and landed *splat* in the mud. His shoes got wrecked, which sucked because they were cool shoes. Worst of all, his best buddy Fischer saw the whole thing. Fischer laughed, so Brobson did too. But he dilly-dallied back to class, all one million of his squishy steps echoing that first humiliating *splat*. Oh so quietly, he said "shit", the way Dad sometimes did when the Steelers had butterfingers.

But how had Mom found out?

"I'm sorry I said a swear," Brobson said from the way back of Mom's Dodge Grand Caravan.

Mom's eyes darted up to the rearview mirror, and back down just as quickly. She was very careful to not take her eyes off of the road. That was probably why she hadn't even looked at him when she'd said the thing about him being born in sin. "When did you say a swear?"

Oh, for golly's…Brobson *thought* a swear, and prayed there was a loophole in that. "I…I didn't. I thought 'heck' was a swear, because I said it in gym, but then I remembered it isn't."

Mom didn't look back up. Brobson cursed his loose tongue twice over and rested his head against the window. The world ticked by outside, a world full of people who were going to go to Hell because they didn't have Moms and Dads to teach them about not sinning.

Then again, Brobson *did* have just such a Mom and Dad, and look how he'd turned out. A let down. He might as well be out there with those other people, saying swears all the live long day.

Except it *wasn't* the swear that Mom was being grumpy about. What else could it be?

Maybe two weeks ago when Fischer pulled out his phone and showed Brobson a video of a naked lady on the internet. Two ladies, to be specific, two ladies rubbing their buttholes together. Brobson couldn't work out which of the two looked more surprised. Fischer thought this was totally sweet, and said so, but Brobson just thought it was all a bit gross. So that shouldn't have been a sin, because it didn't make him feel good, which in his limited experience was the whole point of a sin.

But still, looking at videos on the internet was almost always a sin. If that wasn't literally a Thou Shalt Not in the Bible, it was probably in one of the Expansion Packs Brobson's parents kept buying.

He peeled his head off of the window and opened his mouth to say *I'm sorry I saw two naked ladies rubbing their buttholes together*, but then didn't. He'd already tattled on himself big time by bringing up the swear. And if it *had* been a double-butthole sin Mom was upset about, he'd know. He'd already have been grounded forever, ten times over.

So what the h…what was she mat at him about?

"Did I do something bad, Mom?"

They got all the way to Devonshire before Mom stopped just flitting her eyes to the mirror and actually said something again. "Not yet," she managed. She sounded like she was about to cry, which made Brobson feel even worse.

He couldn't think of anything to say to that – wasn't that good news? – so he let his head fall back onto the window and watched the blur of his neighborhood congeal into a one-story house with a brick façade and cracked tile roof.

Home wasn't nearly as fun as the car. When he looked out his bedroom window, the world didn't move.

DAD CAME HOME from work and didn't say anything. That was weird; for as long as Brobson could remember, Dad would always come home and make all of the noises he was probably not allowed to make at work. He would say "I'm home" in his outside voice, and then drop his suitcase on the cheapo kitchen tiling and make a loud whooping noise like he was at a rock concert (not that any of the Lutz family would ever listen to that kind of music, let alone pay money to stand around with the stinkers who did), then stomp his way over to the living room so he could ask Brobson how his day was, which was annoying because Brobson was somehow *always* at a really interesting part of his book when this happened.

But tonight, Dad didn't say anything. He dropped his suitcase, went upstairs, and came down fifteen minutes later in his around-the-house outfit, slacks and a golf shirt.

Brobson tried to keep reading his book but couldn't, even though it was a really good one about this kid who didn't get Raptured with the rest of his family because he had done too many sins. At least, it had been a really good book yesterday. Today it was too scary.

Mom came downstairs just a minute or two after

Dad. They banged and clanged around the kitchen for a while, and somehow had a spaghetti dinner to show for it. Brobson drifted silently to the dinner table. Mom said Grace. Brobson hoped God could hear *his* little prayers over Mom's.

He and Dad started eating, but Mom just sat there, staring at her food like she was waiting for it to make the first move. Her eyes were getting puffy again. Brobson wanted to say something, but it wasn't his place. Sometimes Mom and Dad got mad at him if he spoke when it wasn't his place.

Mom slid her napkin out from under the silverware and dabbed her lips with it. Either she'd eaten already, or she'd meant to get her eyes and just missed.

Dad hung his head, put down the hearty piece of meatball he'd had halfway to his mouth, and sighed loud enough to drown out the *cling* of the forsaken fork hitting the plate. "Your mother got a call from Father Humphreys about…something that happened earlier this month."

Brobson made a mental list of the sins he'd committed in the month of February. He could remember fourteen. Those were pretty okay numbers, right? He looked to his Mom, who probably only committed like fourteen sins in a whole *year*. No, his numbers were way past okay.

Still, which of the fourteen sins was this about?

Dad looked at Mom. Since Brobson had been looking at Dad, he turned toward her too. She just kept on staring at her plate. An unsettling thought occurred to

Brobson: as long as Mom kept staring at that spaghetti, it would never get cold.

Dad took a deep breath and continued: "We only just found out about it because Ms. McGregor didn't want to notify us prematurely. But she has since felt her initial concerns have been validated."

Ah, there it was: February sin number six. During Social Studies, Ms. McGregor had referred to the Native Americans as "American Indians". Brobson raised his hand because he thought he had heard that was mean to the Native Americans. Ms. McGregor explained that the nomenclature was always in flux, which sounded an awful lot like Science to Brobson.

Was this why Mom and Dad were so upset? He'd raised his hand when it wasn't his place?

"Ms. McGregor," Dad continued with a heavy look towards Mom, "recounted for us an incident that occurred during the St. Valentine's Day celebration, during the exchanging of the cards. Do you remember what happened?"

"Sure," Brobson replied, once again rudderless in the discussion. "We all got to pick our Valentines, who we would make the verse chain with. Er, with whom we would make the verse chain."

"And what happened?"

"I w-"

"Carly asked you to be her St. Valentine," Mom rumbled at her noodles. Had her lips even moved? Or had she simply shaken the Earth with her inexpressible despair, and shaped the words with tectonic plates?

10

"Yeah," Brobson confirmed.

"And you denied her."

"Um, yes, but I swear I – not a, um, I didn't *say* a swear – I mean I *promise* I did it as nice as I could. I wasn't trying to hurt her feelings. I'm sorry if I did. Really," he added, because he meant it.

Mom closed her eyes slower than the sun sets on a bad day. Dad figured that for a tag-in. "Why did you do that?"

Brobson tried to twirl some noodles on his spoon, but gave up. His hands were shaking too much. What had he done? "I just didn't want her to be my Valentine. Everybody was picking the people they liked the best."

Mom snatched back the metaphorical baton by slamming a literal fist on the table. "And who did you ask in her stead?!"

Brobson jumped. "Fischer!"

"Why?"

He looked to Dad, hoping for some of his peace-making magic, but Dad had suddenly gotten very interested in his placemat. Brobson, alone, turned back to his mother. "He's my best buddy!"

"Didn't you notice that all the other boys were asking *girls* to be their St. Valentine?!"

"'Course."

"So why didn't you ask a girl?"

"Because the only person I like enough to be my Valentine is Fischer!"

Mom wailed, burying her head in her hands. Para-

11

lyzed by confusion, Brobson watched as Dad rose from his seat, put his arms around Mom, and spilled his own tears on the shoulder of her dress.

Brobson shrank. He had done this to them. He had wanted Fischer to be his Valentine, which was a sin. He should have known it was a sin; it was something he wanted.

No matter what, he decided that he would never forgive himself. He could only hope that God might. Every night thereafter he prayed for forgiveness, and heard nothing in reply.

TWO

A LOT CHANGED for Brobson after that night, but not nearly as much as he'd expected. The worst of it was not being allowed to hang out with Fischer anymore. The second worst of it was the confiscation of his bicycle, which Brobson had no doubt was done to make sure the first worst of it stuck.

But they couldn't take away his imagination. So, of course, he found ways to see Fischer almost every day. He decided this wasn't a sin because it gave him a tummyache.

"I don't see what the big deal was," Fischer reassured him one unseasonably warm Monday in March. "St. Valentine's Day is dumb anyway."

Brobson had actually been fond of the holiday prior to this year, but kept that to himself. Fischer was older than him by two months, and it was bad to disagree with your elders. "Yeah," Brobson replied, "it is."

"Yeah. Wanna see something cool?" Fischer reached into his pocket and pulled out a lighter, small and silver and definitely a sin for him to have. "I stole it!" he boasted with that devilish smile of his.

Brobson went "aaaah". He couldn't help himself. "From where?"

In one fluid motion, Fischer swung back the lid and struck the flint wheel with his thumb. "Ow," he mumbled as the fun-sized hellfire singed his digit.

"Are you ok?"

"Yeah, yeah. Didn't even feel anything."

Brobson envied the glow caressing Fischer's face. The lighter itself wasn't blowing his mind; he'd seen them before. But he'd never seen one as full of mischievous potential as the flame it bore. It was like Satan's own PEZ dispenser. It terrified and intrigued in equal measure.

Brobson raised his gaze a few inches to see Fischer staring directly at him, eyes glittering. "Cool, right?"

A slow smile trembled along Brobson's face. How many sins was he committing here? Seeing Fischer was one, since his tummy felt better now. Being elated by Fischer's lighter – his *stolen* lighter – that was at least two more. When he got home, he knew his parents would ask him where he'd been, as they always did, and he'd have to tell them a lie. That would be another. Four sins in a single day. But the sins felt so good! Why didn't God make the sins feel bad? Oh, but that was dangerous – disagreeing with God was at least three times as bad as disagreeing with your elders. Probably more.

Shame shot through him, a wintry gasp that smothered the warmth of Fischer's flame. He was breaking his parents' hearts again, staring down the fires of hell and giggling at his own downfall. Maybe Mom was right; maybe Fischer was an emissary of the devil, sent to tempt Brobson into a life of sin and perversion. The lighter wasn't cool; it was evil.

But because Fischer was older, and Mom and Dad's lessons had burrowed in deep, Brobson said "yeah, pretty cool."

THREE

BROBSON STOPPED SEEING Fischer. It wasn't that he didn't want to see his best buddy anymore – he did. That was the problem.

Or, it was part of the problem. What was the problem? He had no idea, but what was clear was that Brobson Lutz *did* have a problem. He knew because Mom loved to kneel down, take him gently by the shoulders and tell him so.

"We can help you," she would often add, although sometimes she wouldn't. Brobson didn't know which was scarier. On the one hand, if he was beyond help, then he would burn in hellfire for all of eternity. He wouldn't be smiling so much *then*, oh no. But on the other hand, he was terrified of how Mom savored the word 'help', like it had a chocolaty center.

As the severity – if not the nature – of the problem

17

was made increasingly clear to Brobson, he found himself more frightened by the one hand than the other. Whatever his chief sin, it frequently reduced his mother to tears, and his father to silent head-shaking, which was basically crying for Men. If something could be done to fix Brobson's problem, maybe it was for the best, whatever it was. That was another thing Mom said sometimes.

By April, the helping had begun. His name was Dr. Lucas, and he had a lot of questions. Since nobody wanted to tell Brobson what was wrong with him outright, he had hoped to work out what his problem was by the kind of treatment it received. Instead, he found himself even more confused after each appointment.

First of all, Dr. Lucas' office was in the back of a church two counties over. Second of all, Dr. Lucas never asked Brobson about his health. He asked him what are your favorite toys to play with, what kinds of sports do you play after school, oh really well do you watch any sports at home, hm, interesting. He asked who are your best friends in school, why do you have so many girls for friends, why didn't you want any of them to be your St. Valentine, ah, fascinating. He gave Brobson little weights and asked him to hold them out straight for ten seconds, no don't let your wrists go limp, *hold* them. That one at least made sense, because doctors love it when their patients are strong.

Over the next few weeks Dr. Lucas became a fixture of Brobson's Tuesday and Thursday evenings, which was fine by him. He wanted to get better so he could

18

stop feeling so miserable and ashamed all the time, and he was glad to have something to take his mind off of Fischer. Which was why it was so frustrating when Fischer was all Dr. Lucas wanted to talk about. Brobson didn't say as much those nights.

This was the weirdest doctor he had ever heard of.

"Dr. Lucas says it's not too late for you," Mom encouraged the rearview mirror one endless Thursday in May. She smiled for the first time in a while. It warmed Brobson's heart, almost as much as Fischer's lighter h-

Now it was Brobson's turn to cry. Why couldn't he stop thinking about Fischer? Dr. Lucas was optimistic about his chances of recovery, but what if he was (but-hesyourelder) *wrong?* What if Brobson Lutz's problem was one that couldn't be solved? What if he couldn't be Saved?

Mom pulled the car over, jumped out, ran around and swung Brobson's door open. She levered herself awkwardly into the wayback and wrapped him up in her arms. "It's not too late for you," she repeated. "We can help you. We can fix you."

"I don't want to go to Hell, Mom."

"You don't have to." She pulled herself away and looked her son square in the eye. It was strange to be in the car and see her actual face, as opposed to its reflection. "You can still make the right choice."

Brobson beat his head hard against the window. When Mom made no motion to stop him, he stopped himself. "I still don't get what my problem is," he mewled between thick, mucusy sniffles.

"That's part of your problem." Mom smiled and tousled his hair before swinging herself out and heading back to the driver's seat.

A few blocks later, she told the mirror to stop crying.

FOUR

HAVING SPENT MOST of his time in the suburbs of Pennsylvania, Brobson had always assumed that Pennsylvania was mostly suburbs. Well, there were cities, like Phoenixville where his cool Aunt Matilda lived, or Philadelphia where America was discovered, but the *rest* of it, Brobson had assumed, was suburbs.

So it was with something approaching awe that, the day after Mom had surprised him with an order to pack his bags for two weeks of summer camp, he watched the familiar world slide out of view from the wayback window of his Mom's Dodge Grand Caravan, to be replaced by more trees than any human had probably ever seen in their entire lives. It was like in movies when they line the criminals up and ask the victim which one of these bad boys did the crime. There were big trees, little trees, fat trees, skinny trees, every kind of

21

tree you could possibly think up – but all of them looked suspicious. Some of the trees were carniver… no, coniferous, and the others were…not. He couldn't remember what those ones were called, but he'd definitely been told.

He wanted to ask Mom or Dad what kind of trees were the ones that weren't Christmas trees, but they were busy Arguing About Directions, which was like I Spy for grown-ups. It didn't sound like as fun a way to pass the time on a long drive, but Mom and Dad were always doing it, so Brobson was probably just too young to understand it.

"…we're *on* 120," Dad snapped at Mom.

"The GPS says we have to turn onto 120. Look. See? *Look*."

"It's probably doing the thing where it gets confused about straightaways."

"This is *all* a straightaway. We're not on 120 yet."

"Yes we *are*!"

Brobson leaned forward, reticent as always to enter the Splash Zone. "Dad?"

Mom flitted her eyes to the mirror, then back to the road. She shook her head. "So I guess you know better than the GPS. You know better than the space satellite."

Dad chuckled like a volcano. "No, you're right, the camera a million miles in the sky knows these roads better than I do. You must be right."

"Mom?"

"Ok, well, if we're on 120, why did I just see an exit

for Lock Haven?"

"*Because*," Dad exploded like a bigger volcano that hadn't gotten any sacrifices lately, "I know what you're going to say but that's because you can get to Lewistown from the 644 *or the 120.*"

"So you admit we could be on the 6-"

"Dad?"

Dad said "UGH" to Mom like a volcano deciding to retire and become a mountain, and turned around to Brobson. "What?"

Brobson flinched slightly, as he had been doing for the past month or so whenever he saw his parents' eyes. It felt like he was watching a school assembly and suddenly the spotlight fell on *him*. What was he supposed to do?

Oh, that's right. "Um, what do they call those trees that don't look like Christmas trees?"

"Coniferous trees."

Mom shook her head. "Those *are* the ones that lo-"

"I *know*, I was just telling him what they were. The other ones are deciduous trees."

Brobson looked out the window for a moment, trying to keep all of the trees straight. He turned back to Dad. "Wait, which one is which?"

"It's not important," said the back of Dad's head.

Sighing quietly, Brobson returned his attention to the lineup.

FIVE

NINETY MINUTES AND infinity trees later, they pulled off the highway onto a narrow dirt road. Branches with thick, flat leaves (Brobson wasn't about to speculate on which sort of tree these belonged to) arced over the uneven trail, hiding travelers from the sun – or maybe the opposite. For at least twenty minutes they bounced and jounced their way deeper into the wood, slowly and none too surely. It was as though the forest was playing the part of a good host, parting before them, inviting them in, only to quietly seal itself up behind them.

Brobson *knew* the trees had looked suspicious.

Finally, they rounded a corner and came upon a little shack in the center of the road. Standing as tall as it could between two barrier gates, it struck a whimsical figure, which was certainly not what Brobson would have expected from security at a camp as prestigious as

25

First Stone. What he *had* expected were the two very scary looking guards pacing around, now talking into their wrists and waving Mom up to the booth. The guards didn't have guns in their hands, and they looked really upset about it. Neither smiled or said howdy as they positioned themselves on either side of the car.

Dad shot Brobson a strange look. It was one that contained a wealth of knowledge Brobson would acquire, at great personal expense, over the coming weeks.

Mom pulled up to the booth and smiled at the tollbooth operator, who exploded. "Blessing!" he screamed. Brobson could suddenly understand why the other two guys out there were frowning so much. "How are you on this glorious day?"

"I'm f…we're fine," Mom managed.

"That's just terrific. So, what brings you out here this morning, Mrs…"

"Lutz."

"Lutz, Mrs. Lutz, it's wonderful to meet you."

"And you as well, Mr…"

"Ted, just Ted will do us right."

Mom nodded her head. "Ted it is, then."

A breeze rattled the trees. A bird squawked once, then got self-conscious.

"So," Ted resumed, "what brings you out here, Mrs. Lutz?"

"Oh, right. We're here to drop our son off."

"Ah!" Ted leaned in to the car, head darting from side to side like a cat in front of a fish tank. His eyes settled upon Brobson. "A-ha. This is Brobson, then?"

Brobson flinched. "How do you know my name?"

Ted tapped his temple. "The list, my good man. Your name is on the list! You can call me Teddy, if you like."

"Um, thank you."

Ted's smile remained the same size, but somehow it also got very, very small. "Now's your chance, kiddo. We won't see each other again until Mom and Dad come and pick you up!" *THWONG*, he slapped the roof hard with an open palm. Brobson jumped, the seatbelt catching across his shoulder.

"You're gonna go straight through here," Ted told Mom with as many hand gestures as he could manage, "take a right. Stick on that for about a half mile, then it'll open right up and you'll see a big pavilion. There's a gravel road that swings 'round the whole thing, just drop him anywhere on that." He punched a button in his booth. The booth buzzed in protest. The arm of the gate ratcheted upwards, which still felt pretty silly against the natural, terrible majesty of the wilderness. So it was a good thing for First Stone they had those two bicep monsters to keep the tone suitably intimidating.

"Last chance to call me Teddy, Brobson!" he called into the car as Mom shifted into drive. Brobson said nothing, to which Teddy shrugged and chuckled "alright pal, see you in August!"

The car started forward, and Brobson's heart stopped. "August?"

Mom and Dad stared straight out the front windshield. "I think..." Mom mumbled, "...said...right?"

27

"Yeah…" Dad whispered, "right."

So they were *definitely* just ignoring him; there was no other explanation for their agreeing about which way to go. "I thought I was only going for two weeks! That's what you said!"

Mom cranked the steering wheel and squinted out the windshield. After a moment or two, she grumbled about how most kids would be over the moon about going to summer camp at all, let alone for three months.

"But I…" he couldn't well say he didn't want to be away from Fischer for that whole time, since he hadn't been supposed to be near him to begin with, and anyway, he'd been avoiding him. But the fact was, there was still something nice about knowing he *could* see his best buddy any time he wanted, even if he didn't. "Why'd you tell me two weeks then?"

"They can help you here," Dad assured the dashboard. "They can make you better."

Oh brother. Had they brought him out here, a million miles from nowhere, to spend three months being asked what his favorite toys were? "I thought Dr. Lucas was helping me," he very judiciously offered.

"Dr. Lucas was helping *us* figure out how best to help *you*. We've determined that you can best be helped by the people here."

Brobson looked at his Dad, head cocked slightly sideways. He had thought this was just going to be a regular old summer camp, one they were sending him to just to keep him away from Fischer. This was a pretty lame change of plans, but all the same…he needed help. He was broken, and broken things needed to be fixed. They needed to be fixed while they still *could* be fixed.

And if they really could put Broken Brobson back together again here, wasn't that worth three months of his life? Three months to deliver him from the eternal torments of Hell? That was a no-brainer, really.

So he settled back into his seat, unhappy but resigned, and marveled at his Mom's ability to maintain her sense of direction in this crush of leaves and timber. Brobson couldn't begin to tell which way was which.

SIX

ONE SMALL CONSOLATION was that Mom and Dad seemed genuinely sad when they dropped him off. They left him on the gravel, just as Ted had instructed them. As the car crunched its way back to the dirt road cleft into the forest, Brobson made a mental note of how much he was not crying. It wasn't a conscious decision, and it was even a little bit off-putting. But there he stood, eyes dry as last summer's waterproof watch just before he dunked it in the pool and discovered the difference between a promise and a fact.

In the flurry of gestures and directions, Ted had neglected to mention what Brobson was supposed to do now, or where he was supposed to go. He looked around for any helpful signage. He saw exactly two signs. The first said:

31

THURSDAY NIGHT IS TALENT NIGHT!
SIGN-UP SHEETS CAN BE FOUND IN THE NURSE'S CABIN

Which was kind of helpful, except for Brobson didn't have any talents. The second said:

THE WICKED SHALL BE TURNED INTO HELL
PSALM 9:17

Which was kind of helpful, except it made it sound like the wicked would be transformed into Hell itself. Which didn't really make sense, but Brobson also hadn't known that sin was a place, so who was he to be confused by a Bible verse?

The first sign was hanging from the spacious central pavilion, about the size of his church's nave, except instead of big stained glass windows and a pointy cave ceiling it was just an oversized white barn roof balanced on big red stilts. Beneath was a concrete floor that bucked up its act at the far end and became a concrete stage, on which there was a drumset and a load of amplifiers.

From this central pavilion, the rest of the camp stretched in all directions. On Brobson's side of the pavilion (away from the stage), there sat a squat but formidable concrete structure at the crest of a low hill, which sloped gently down to a small wooden cabin about the size of the singlewide behind the school where Coach Duffy lived. Branching out from the gravel of the road, a wide dirt thoroughfare snaked into the looming wood.

On the other side of the camp, past the graceless

32

stage, an unkempt yard sprawled over itself like it had just fallen off a ladder.

A few big kids in all black were in the yard, just standing around, too far from each other to talk but close enough to be *together*.

Seeing no one else, Brobson walked over to those strange kids, taking the long way around the pavilion. Even though there was nothing to stop him from cutting through, he somehow knew that he would be breaking a rule if he did.

As the gravel gave way to the librarian's hush of the grass, Brobson began to revise his assessment of these five kids. For starters, they were adults – parents, he was almost certain. It wasn't just the way the soft flesh hung haphazardly on their frames, as though hurled at them from a great distance. It was their silent authority, their embodied sense of unmet expectations.

With each step he took, the world grew less talkative. Birds stopped singing. The trees stopped sighing. Even the windchimes on that wooden cabin across the stage fell silent, as Brobson approached the first of the five not-just-parents-but-*dads* standing in the field. All dressed head-to-toe in thick black robes, which was sort of intimidating but mostly baffling because it was a scorcher of a day. Maybe that was why the cloth was hugging their lumpy frames like that. Brobson was sweating, and he was in shorts and a T-shirt; these poor dads must have been *drenched*. Most puzzling of all, each clutched a tall wooden staff, like a quintet of depressed Moses lookalikes.

Brobson approached the first Staff Dad and lifted his eyes as far as the man's chin. "Um," he began, "I'm a n-"

"What is a man?" The man boomed.

Oh, no. This *was* going to be like working with Dr. Lucas.

"Um…a man is…a grown-up boy?"

The dad in black nodded and gestured to the second dad, just behind him. Brobson puzzled over this. If one thought of the five dads as a trail of breadcrumbs, then they led straight to…nothing. And yet, he was being told to follow the fathers. Where to? It was hardly worth pondering; they would tell him when he got there.

"What does it mean to *be* a man?" asked Staff Dad 2.

Brobson shrugged. He wasn't sure how he was supposed to know, seeing as he was just a boy. Had they taught this in school and he'd just forgotten, like the times tables? Must have – they wouldn't be asking him something he wasn't supposed to know the answer to. God, why didn't he ever pay attention?

"Being a man is…being an adult. Making sure your family is safe."

Onwards to Staff Dad Number 3: "How does one become a man?"

"By…getting older? You have to get a good job too."

This was starting to feel like if Dr. Lucas designed one of those theme rides at the carnival. Grab your sweetie for The Tunnel of Love, face your fears in the

Hall of Horrors, scratch your head in the Field of Fathers!

Speaking of, here was Father the Fourth: "What is more important than being a man?"

"…nothing?" Unsure of what would be expected of him after fielding (ha) the final question, he took his time strolling up to the Fifth Father.

This last dad leaned over, bending not at the knees like a loving uncle but from the waist, like he was scolding a dog. "Why can't *you* be a man?" he snarled.

Brobson thought he *could* be a man, some day. Why couldn't he be a man? This was news to him! "Because I'm not old enough?" he hoped out loud.

"Why can't you *ever* be a man?"

To this, Brobson was speechless. He couldn't *ever* be a man? What was wrong with him?!

The Fifth Staff Dad lifted his wooden staff and pointed back towards where Brobson had just come from, towards the central pavilion. Brobson hoped against hope he would see a flying lawnmower or something, and that's how he would find out that this was a camp for wizards, and his parents had known all along and now he was going to learn how to be a wizard. Instead, he saw the four other dads with their backs to him. No more words were exchanged, and no further gestures were made. For lack of alternatives, Brobson set off in the indicated direction.

He was neither man nor wizard; what did that leave?

SEVEN

PAST THE PAVILION, across the gravel, onto the wide path. This was the way the man with the staff had pointed, and so this was the way Brobson went.

That path led him to a shaded hollow, the tranquility of which couldn't quite disguise the sustained violence of its creation. *Nature* certainly hadn't looked upon the quiet majesty of this grove and decided to cookie-cut a big hole out of it.

Within this space, eight cabins had been erected, organized into four pairs. Those pairs each shared a single patio between the two of them, which was about the right size for one person to breakdance on if they weren't afraid of splinters.

The four pairs were situated in what looked like a very deliberate way, maybe the four cardinal directions. All four faced inward, towards a rather sad little pile of rocks and sticks that probably wanted to be a fire pit when it grew up. Brobson wondered what it was like, having that kind of direction in life.

"Ahoy!" came a voice from the thicket.

Brobson started and spun on his heel. He had no clue where the voice was coming from, but heel-spinning was a reaction that felt natural and appropriate.

"I'm in…hang on!" the voice called. There was a loud *BANG* to Brobson's right, which necessitated another spin, albeit a slightly more targeted one.

"Sorry," said the man standing in the now-open doorway of the cabin on the…from the…well now Brobson was facing it so it was in front of him, and that was as specific an orientation as he could manage.

Come to think of it, which way did he even come into this clearing from?

"I forgot you wouldn't be able to see me from out here." The cabin man waved a clipboard around as he spoke. He was more animated than most men with clipboards that Brobson had ever seen. "I was in the cabin," he added, in case Brobson had imagined he materialized from a different dimension.

"Oh, ha ha," Brobson said. "Um, am I supposed to be h-"

"Yes!" the man slapped his clipboard. He was…Old. Brobson wasn't very good at guessing ages; if they weren't Young, they were either Old or Ancient. This Old guy wasn't Ancient, and might not have been Young all that long ago. But he was still Old. "Yes, of course! I'm Hal," he announced as he bounced down the two wooden steps and across the dirt to Brobson. "And you must be Brobson Lutz!" Hal consulted his clipboard, and nodded once. "Yeah! Right?"

Had Brobson wandered in to a different camp by accident? Surely the same company couldn't employ Hal *and* the Five Freaky Field Fathers. How could they share a break room?

And yet, Hal had Brobson's name on a clipboard. That meant something.

"That's right." Getting into the spirit of camp, he added "Sir."

Hal looked genuinely shocked. He smiled, but it wasn't the happiest smile Brobson had ever seen. "You don't have to 'sir' me, man. I'm just the junior counselor. Some of the other counselors really go in for that 'sir' stuff, though." Hal's face didn't change, and yet his smile expanded.

Brobson couldn't help it: he smiled too. Gosh, how long had it been since he'd really felt comfortable talking to…well, anybody?

Hal clapped him on the shoulder, the way Brobson imagined a big brother or a proud father would. "The other boys are on a little nature walk right now. What do you say I give you the grand tour?"

"That'd be really nice."

"That how you talk to your buddies, Brobson? 'That'd be really nice?'" Hal said this not in a bullying tone (Brobson was certain of this, for his was a well-tuned ear), but in the way of, yes, a buddy.

Granted, Brobson wasn't about to talk to Hal exactly

as he would one of his friends, since the way he'd talked to one of his friends was why he'd been sent here in the first place…but he could try to loosen up.

"No," Brobson chuckled, "it's not."

Hal waved his clipboard around some more. "Yeah! Soooo, the grand tour? Whaddaya say?"

"Sweet!"

Hal laughed. "There he is!"

Brobson laughed too. He could hardly remember the dread he'd felt on the drive up here; now, he was mostly worried about three months with Hal not being *enough*. Those Staff Dads were weird, but approachable enough in their slightly-scary-Muppet way. They'd be easy to avoid. If First Stone was full of Hals, though, this was going to be the best summer of Brobson's life.

Laughing together, Hal and Brobson made their way back towards the central campground. Before long, the forest swallowed up their voices, and the echoes bled into the Earth.

EIGHT

ROBSON SAW IT all: the showers (that big concrete structure at the top of the hill), the dining hall (which he hadn't seen on his first stroll, plopped on the far side of the steep mount upon which First Stone was located), and the nurse's cabin (the smaller wooden structure near the stage). And, really, that was all of it. Oh, and the pavilion of course, which was impossible to miss. That was where they had the events and songs and everything. There was a pretty important one tonight, Hal told Brobson, though he didn't seem over the moon about it. Therefore, Brobson was similarly unenthused.

Brobson stuck close to Hal, as the tour hadn't done much for his sense of direction.

"Ah!" Hal exclaimed as they returned to the clearing with the cabins that had a really weird name, which conveniently sounded like *Guessthename*, which Brobson could not. "They're back!"

41

And so they were: the hole in the forest was full of kids. But no livelier for it. The boys, all around Brobson's age, were absorbed in solitary pursuits; reading, writing, drawing. The adventurous ones played cards with a partner. And strolling among them like a general surveying his troops was "Rowan," Hal whispered to Brobson. "Head counselor."

Rowan turned slowly towards Brobson, evidently not liking what he was seeing. This look intensified when he finished turning and actually *saw* Brobson. He shot his eyes towards Hal. Back to Brobson.

"Where's your bag?" Rowan asked.

"My what?" Brobson asked back.

Rowan's face went as red as a rash. "Your what, *what?*"

Brobson considered this. "I don't know?"

"*Sir*," Hal muttered out of the side of his mouth.

Inhaling sharply, Rowan turned to Hal. "Don't assist him!"

"Sorry, sir," Hal said as he lowered his head. "Brobson's bag was left in the visitor's center by his parents. Standard procedure, sir." Hal winked. Brobson smiled.

Satisfied, Rowan returned his stony attentions to Brobson, who had tucked his smile away for safekeeping. "You are lodging in the South complex. Cabin three, bunk six. We are currently experiencing a period known as 'free time'. This lapses at five o'clock PM, at which point you are expected at the mess. Following your meal, a presentation will occur at the central pavilion at seven o'clock PM. Attendance is mandatory. If at any point you find yourself unsure of where to go, simply follow one of the other boys. Do you understand?"

Brobson's eyes drifted around the campground. Some of the other boys were looking up at him, but most kept their eyes locked on their chosen activities. Brobson got the sense that they were all listening, though.

"I asked you a question," Rowan snapped like a rope bridge.

"Yes, I understand."

Rowan grimaced.

Brobson flinched. "Sir! I got it, sir. I mean, I understand. Sir."

"Alright," Rowan allowed. He waved Brobson away and turned back around, to look disapprovingly at nothing in particular.

Each of the four cabin pairs looked identical to Brobson. Once again, First Stone was notable for a lack of helpful signage. Brobson looked up to Hal imploringly.

Thank heavens, Hal graced him with a smile (albeit one tempered by a quick glance towards Rowan). He led Brobson away from the dreadful head counselor. "Look," he said, pointing towards one of the cabin pairs. "That's the south, uh, *complex*. Do you know how I can tell that?"

"Because...because you've been working here a long time?"

Hal made a cartoonishly large 'you've got it' face,

43

which he immediately followed up with a hard "no". Brobson had to stifle his laugh – this did not seem like a space that had ever been sullied by a snicker. "I might as well have started yesterday. I'm the new blood, like you. No, I can tell it's south because of that." Hal pointed to a tree, indistinguishable from any other tree. "See what's notable about that tree?"

"No."

"How about…" his finger, and so Brobson's gaze, swung to the left. "How about that one?"

"It's just a tree."

Hal sighed patiently, which reminded Brobson that as much fun as Hal might have been, he was still Old. "See how the moss grows on it?"

"Yeah. The green stuff."

"The green stuff, that's right. Now look back at *that* tree."

"Okay. There's moss on that one too."

"What do you notice?"

"…" Brobson squinted, as he wanted Hal to know he really was thinking about this. "…oh! It's growing on the same side!"

"Exactly. Moss grows on the north side of trees. Go away from the moss, and you'll find your cabin."

"Oh. Cool!" He looked at the pair of cabins. "But how do I know wh-"

"Cabin three is on the left. That one you just have to remember."

"Ok."

Hal went off to do the duties of the Old, leaving

Brobson to his own devices. He took a peek into his cabin, and found his bunk – he knew it not because it was labeled, but because it was empty.

"Lutz!" Rowan shouted from outside. "Pass the time where God can see you!"

This was the first Brobson had heard of God's inability to see through ceilings, but he complied without comment. Lacking access to the books he'd crammed into his bag, which was helpfully locked up on the other side of the compound, Brobson spent the remainder of free time sitting on an inviting patch of dirt and staring at the sky.

NINE

ASSURED HIS BAG would be waiting for him when he returned to his cabin that evening, Brobson followed the other boys to dinner. The mess hall was exactly what the name promised, a soggy hut with two long tables and benches to match. Sunlight pounded vainly on the grease-smeared windows, eventually giving up and heading west. If this little shack had been around when God flooded the world so Noah could take a cruise (which based on the condition it may well have been), Brobson couldn't imagine it looking any different for being at the bottom of a deep, vengeful ocean.

The food wasn't very good, either.

Still, he said thank you to the frog-woman in the hairnet and sat down at the first open seat he found. In short order, four other kids sat down, apparently a group of friends.

"Hi," one of them said to Brobson before he'd hardly touched butt to bench. "are you here on purpose?" The boy's three compatriots leaned in.

"Oh, hi?" Brobson blinked. "Hi. I don't think so. My mom made me c-"

All four of Brobson's unexpected guests made relieved noises.

"What's your name?" the apparent leader of the quartet asked.

"Brobson. What's yours?"

"Ned. Do you have a nickname?"

"No."

Ned nodded. His hair was long and floppy, and as he nodded the brown locks smacked his freckled face like they wanted his lunch money. "Some people are here on purpose. The older ones. They're stupid."

"Well," Brobson reiterated, "my mom sent me here."

"My stepdad sent me." Ned's eyes bugged out like he'd realized he left his phone at home (which, of course, he'd have had to – camp rules). "These are my friends," he added with a sudden jerk of the head. He followed it up with a point to the tallest of his friends. "That's Fred. It's annoying that our names sound the same, but he's really tall which is cool."

"What's up," Fred asked Brobson rhetorically from the stratosphere. Ned was right; Fred *was* cool.

Brobson, always happy for low-hanging conversational fruit, plucked the first thing that came to mind. "You know the guy who sits in the little booth out

48

front is named Ted?"

"*Ugh*," said Ned and Fred.

The cherub with glittery cheeks next to Fred chimed in: "I heard they have guns there, and they shoot kids who try to run away."

"You can't shoot kids," sighed the ginger boy sitting next to Ned. "It's illegal."

"The police shoot kids all the time!"

"Well, that's different. My dad says those were all bad kids who should have just listened."

Ned shook his head, much to the evident displeasure of his hair. "That's Quazi and Scott. They're always arguing. Fred thinks it's because they want to kiss each other."

"I'll kiss Scott," Quazi leered. "I kissed a girl *and* a boy already. Might as well kiss a ginger!"

Scott looked to his left, and then to his right. He looked behind him, and then under his seat. Then, and only then, did he shoot Quazi the middle finger. As quickly as it appeared, it vanished.

"Quazi likes girls and boys, but his parents only care about he likes boys," Ned explained.

At the bottom of Brobson's stomach, an ancient sea creature stirred. It was something massive, something that had passed its whole life in slumber.

Brobson turned to Quazi, currently making wet smoochy faces at Scott. "Why do they call you Quazi?"

"Like Quazimodo, from the movie."

"Yeah, but like, *why*?"

Quazi shrugged his two decidedly normal shoulders.

"It's kind of like an inside joke with kids at my school, I guess."

Scott shook his head. "It's because he's a freak."

Quazi blew him a kiss. Scott wretched. Fred smiled down upon the scene.

Compared to his three friends, Ned behaved like a chaperone with a mischievous streak. He stirred the pot and stood back. "Scott likes boys but doesn't want to admit it."

Fred and Quazi leaned towards Scott, expectant smiles on their faces.

Scott grimaced at Brobson. "I used to say 'no I don't', but then they just say ex-"

"Exactly!" Fred and Quazi shouted in unison.

"QUIET!" Rowan screamed from the other side of the mess.

Brobson's four new friends ducked their heads down in unison, and kept them lowered for a second or two longer than was strictly necessary. During this interlude, Brobson poked at the slop on his plate, and once again made the decision not to bother with it. "How long have you guys been here?"

Ned, as usual, responded immediately. "I've been here since three days ago. Fred's been here longest of anybody. It's why he's so quiet, is because he's seen it all."

Fred nodded sagaciously.

Brobson craned his neck up. "How long?"

Staring through the cabin and into the expanse of the past, Fred steeled himself and responded "six days."

50

Everyone at the table shuddered.

"I've been here three days," Scott said. "Quazi's been h-"

"Quazi can answer for himself," Quazi cut in. "Qu...I got here on Saturday. What day is it?"

"Monday," Brobson informed him with a hint of despair. He didn't know?

"There you go. Saturday Sunday Monday."

"What's it like here? My mom didn't really tell me, just said they were gonna m-"

"Make you not gay?" Fred scoffed.

The ancient sea creature rumbled from the depths, looked at its ancient sea clock and blooped out bubbles that spelled AW JEEZ.

"No," Brobson insisted with an unfortunate crack in his voice. "No, I'm not gay."

Scott raised out of his seat, opening his mouth to exclaim something. He took a quick glance around and lowered back down. "See?" he hissed at Ned. "Lots of people say they aren't gay."

"Don't you like boys?" Fred asked Brobson.

Brobson wrinkled his nose. "No!"

"So you like girls, then?"

"Yeah. Lots of my friends are girls."

The four shot each other knowing looks. Even Scott, which Brobson thought was pretty darn rich.

"I'm not gay," he reiterated as the ancient sea creature hastily threw on its jacket and shoes and rushed out the ancient sea door. "I can't be gay, because if I were gay then I would be..."

The ancient sea creature arose from its cave, into penetrating shafts of daylight.

He would be broken. Broken in a way that *couldn't* be fixed.

He would be turned in to Hell itself.

Ned put a hand on Brobson's shoulder, which Brobson instinctively shook off. "Are *you* gay?" he asked defensively.

"Everybody here is gay, dude. It is First Stone, after all." He gave Brobson a wink. Did Ned get that from Hal, or vice versa? Or had they both become winkers independently?

Brobson's face must have fallen hard, because Ned suddenly looked quite serious. "Do you not know what First Stone is?"

"Are they gonna try to make us not be…" Brobson waved his hand in front of him. "You know…"

"Yeah. And do you know how they do that?"

"…prayer?"

Ned probably thought Brobson didn't see the anxious eyes he shot to his three friends. But Brobson saw, alright.

TEN

BROBSON WALKED TO the pavilion with his four new friends. Brobson said things, and he listened to the things that they said in response, and he in turn said more things that built upon those things that they had said.

But he wasn't really listening, to them or to himself. All he could hear, all he could fix in his mind, was a single word, repeated over and over.

Ordeals.

That was what Ned had said, and Fred the veteran had confirmed it. Quazi and Scott, newbies though they were, both unhappily echoed the sentiment.

Ordeals. It was such a...*specific* word. That was maybe what disturbed Brobson the most about it.

They all filed into the pavilion, lit up like a baseball stadium. Maybe somebody had made that comparison out loud, or maybe it had just popped up in some muted quarter of Brobson's mind. It hardly mattered.

What mattered, Brobson thought as he and his new buddies joined the crush of boys pressing towards the stage, was what Quazi had said. That in the papers their parents signed before sending them to camp, there was something that said that the counselors could hurt their kids if they thought it was essential for their "therapy". He said that the parents were told about that part specifically, and it was on its own page they had to sign.

What mattered was that, unlike with Quazi's assertion that the bicep monsters at the booth were armed (which Brobson was fairly sure wasn't true), Scott didn't say anything to contradict him on the permission slip thing. And according to Ned, those two were *always* arguing.

Was this why Mom and Dad had been so quiet around him, and looked so uncomfortable on the drive up? Was this why they'd made a point of reminding him how much they (apparently) loved him before saying goodbye?

A place where parents sent their children to be hurt couldn't be allowed, could it?

Just as he opened his mouth to put this question to Scott, who seemed to know the most about stuff that was and wasn't allowed, the lights over the boys dimmed and Rowan marched up onto the stage, snatching the microphone like he'd just lost a bet.

"Alright boys," he mumbled. Despite the terrible reputation this man had amongst Ned and his crew (and presumably all of the boys) as being someone for whom the switch was always near at hand, Brobson

54

found it oddly poignant to see that he was uncomfortable with his own amplified voice. "This evening we have a most unexpected guest who wishes to discuss your lamentable decisions with you. Many of you are likely familiar with him, either because you yourselves have viewed his television program, or else your parents have, and you were perhaps present in the room but distracted by any number of the things liable to distract an undisciplined mind. In addition to his renown, of course, our guest tonight was one of the key investors in First Stone. This is the time for applause." Rowan walked away from the microphone, halted mid-step, and lunged back.

"I've completely forgotten," he added, "the guest of whom I speak is the Reverend Dr. Keith Malamar." He leaned over his captive audience and slapped his hands together. The boys got the idea and joined in, which was good enough for Rowan. As the head counselor was practically diving off of the stage, another man ascended.

This man wasn't uncomfortable under the merciless spotlights, no sir. If anything, as he wrapped a delicate hand around the microphone and brought it close to his parted, upturned lips, he looked like a man who'd wheel in his own personal spotlights if the venue in question couldn't provide. He wore a suit as white as fresh snowfall, which Brobson thought was an unspeakably courageous thing to do – it was tantamount to wearing a shirt that said *I Will Not Be Spilling Anything Today*. His skin wasn't quite that white – it had seen the business end of too many spray tans to be – but it wasn't far off. The man smiled at the microphone, and his teeth glinted at exactly the same time as the feedback screeched.

"Well, thank you for such a...*fabulous* introduction, Mr. Monteagle," the Reverend Doctor cooed like a foul-tempered pigeon. "It does my heart good to see so many youngsters, led astray from the path, being guided back by the light of fine pastoral care."

Brobson had no idea what Malamar was talking about, but it was a familiar patter. Mom and Dad had watched his show, "Crossroads with Reverend Dr. Keith Malamar", on Sunday afternoons, broadcast live from his Megachurch somewhere in the South. Each episode featured a lengthy sermon, followed by the audience participation section, when people in wheelchairs rolled up to get bonked on the head by the Reverend Doctor's Bible so that they could do cartwheels over to the donations bucket. Every once in a while there were exorcisms performed Live On Stage, which were always kind of disappointing because you never got to actually see the demon. It was just some old lady doing some bad scat until she, too, got bonked by a Bible.

To see the Reverend Doctor in the flesh was disorienting, and Brobson got the sense he wasn't alone in having that reaction. There was a lot of corner-eye activity going on in the pit, which didn't escape the headliner's notice.

"Yes, yes, it really is me. And surely you're wondering what is the purpose of my visit. If you'll bow your heads and silence yourselves, I shall enlighten you." He waited impatiently until this was accomplished. "There, I trust you can all hear me better now, yes? Of course." He plucked the mic from its stand and took it for a walk. "Let's begin with a prayer. Dear God, thank You for the truth of Yours that will be deposited in our lives. Thank You for Your Spirit and Your Grace which You pour out upon Your Chosen each day, as You have for the last two thousand years. And thank You for the change and the transformation that will make these boys into Men who deserve their place in Your world, as we hear the Word and act on Your Word, that we will be the Doers of the Same. And everyone shouted Amen!"

"Amen," the more intuitive of the boys echoed.

"I am here to talk to you about sin," Malamar thundered, his voice finishing a half-octave lower than where it began. "S-I-N, sin. What is sin? Is it a confusion? A simple misunderstanding, is that what sin is? Or is it a *choice*, a decision you make daily?" Malamar paused. A camper just in front of the stage raised their hand. The Reverend Doctor shooed the hand away.

"I've traveled all over God's creation, spreading the Good Word. And I *don't* just mean with my highly rated television broadcast, or my wildly successful podcast. No, boys, I mean bodily, transported bodily through the air to new lands, savage and hungry for Salvation." He stopped and smiled sheepishly at the air, as he often did on television. After several seconds of silence, he resumed as though there had been no pause. Brobson was put in mind of his Uncle Pat.

Uncle Pat would do that same thing, where he would just freeze while his eyes ran laps around his head. Sometimes in the middle of a story. If you asked him why he'd turned into a statue for a few seconds, he'd look at you like *you* were the weirdo. Turned out Uncle Pat had epilepsy, and those were little seizures he was having. Poor Uncle Pat. Rest in peace.

"And do you know what I found," Malamar continued, "visiting with everyone from the highest Church officials to the lowliest slum dweller? Do you? I found that those who suffer...smile." Malamar demonstrated the latter half of the maxim, running his fingers up his cheeks. The smile collapsed under its own weight. "Jesus calls us not simply to believe in Him, but to suffer for His name, Amen."

"Amen," said that little brownnoser who'd raised his hand earlier.

"It is not enough to profess belief. You must live your faith." He dug a manicured hand into the starchy collar of his shirt and fished. "I...you see...hang on..." Eyes alight, he yanked a golden chain from beneath his glorious modesty. "Ah! You see, this is why I have done quite well to repopularize this symbol." The symbol in question was a golden cross dangling from the end of his chain. The harsh stagelights captured a rogue chest hair that had been torn off in the brandishing maneuver. "We have lost sight of how Jesus suffered for us, but you know who hasn't? *Jesus*. He said that if you lose your life for my sake, you will find it. *His* sake, I mean, of course. Ha, ha. Amen."

Everyone recognized this as a rhetorical Amen.

"How is there to be *power* in belief, if it is servicing a faith of *softness?* Belief is *power* – or at least it *was*, before the effeminizing influence of rock music and car chase films turned this," Malamar said as he stuck a tightly clenched fist straight out in front of him, "into this." His hand flopped open, his wrist hanging limply. "The weak and womanly succumb to temptation. Why? Because it is *easy*. Because it is *popular*. Because it *feels good*. But at what cost?"

Malamar paused again, and trotted over to a water bottle tucked next to a speaker. He opened it and frowned. He looked off stage. Back at the water bottle. "Now here is an example. This water bottle is already open," he announced as he shot somebody just off stage a *very* nasty look, "which leaves me two choices. I can refuse to drink the water, demanding only the *purest* water, only my *favorite* kind of water. Or I can *man up*, and drink the water offered to me by Providence and the incompetence of humankind. Even though it's already open." He breathed in through his nose and threw back the bottle, taking a hearty swig of the potentially contaminated water.

"Ah!" he shouted. "How refreshing! And you see, I have sated my thirst, and so put a smile upon my face, by making the decision to be a Man. I certainly could have turned from the Call, and demanded a *fresh water bottle* that *hasn't been opened already*." Another flower-wilting glare off stage. "But had I done that, my thirst

59

would have become greater, as it would have taken more time for a new bottle to be fetched for me. Do you understand? Of course not."

Brobson was relieved to hear that he didn't understand, because he *didn't* understand. Malamar's sermons had always confused him when he saw them on TV, but this was the most baffling one yet.

"Homosexuality is an abomination," Malamar explained as a stagehand rushed up with a fresh bottle of water. The Reverend Doctor handed off the opened bottle without turning his face from the crowd. "It is the very bottom of the Bottomless Pit, the final temptation to which only the *weakest* succumb. First Corinthians says that the unrighteous shall *not* inherit the Kingdom of God. The types thereof are then listed, and do you know where the homosexuals land? Just between *adulterers* and *thieves*." He cracked open his new water bottle, stealing a glance at his Oreo-sized watch as he did.

"Now, I want to make something *perfectly* clear to you: nobody is *born* gay. They've done studies, and tests. And how much evidence is there that this condition is genetic? How many scientists have been able to demonstrate that homosexuality is biological?" He took a swig of water. "*None*. Absolutely *zero*. Not a *one*." He screwed the cap back on the bottle.

"So from whence this…*malady?* Well, the first thing to know is that it is uniquely human. I mentioned my travels across the globe. I have seen the wildlife in every country on Earth; the monkeys in Brazil. The elephants

60

in India. The lions in Africa. I once saw a herd of gazelle, and do you know what? Only one of them had horns. One male, to seventy-five females. Those are good odds! Ha, ha. Amen.

"But seriously kids, do you know how many times I saw two gazelle lying together, both with horns? How many heavily-maned lions I saw mounting each other? How many pretty peacocks I saw putting their unmentionables in each other's mouths? *None.* Absolutely *zero.* Not a *one.* And believe me: I was looking. But homosexuality exists in our accursed race, and *only* in ours. That is because it is a *decision* that could only be made by a race cast out from the garden, a race capable of plucking the forbidden fruit for no other reason than it was *forbidden.*"

Malamar paused yet again, looking up and to the left. Brobson followed his gaze, but didn't see anything. After a moment, the Reverend Doctor shook his head and continued his stroll around the stage. "Homosexuality is a deviant behavior that stems from childhood deprivations. A-A-A, those are three As for you to remember." He raised the pointer finger of his left hand. "Attention." The middle finger went up. "Affection." The third finger followed suit. "Affirmation." The fingers fell penitently into a claw, which returned to the cap of the water bottle. "Those who lack the three 'A's from their parents also probably suffer sexual abuse. They cannot make new friends, nor keep old ones. And so, having failed to understand the basics of human interaction, they adopt what the liberal media calls a 'gender identity'." He made air quotes, spilling some water from the bottle as he did. If he noticed, he didn't let on. A consummate professional.

"And then what? Boys, lacking proper father figures, put penises in their mouths. When that is what God made Woman for! You *cannot* be a *Man* with a penis in your mouth. To give is *strength*, you understand. To receive, *weakness*. You understand?"

Brobson still didn't, and hoped that nobody else did either. He had never put a penis in his mouth, and was somewhat disgusted by the very idea of it. Penises were where you pissed out of (that was where the word "piss" came from – it was "penis" in a hurry). He did, however, find the word 'penis' to be funny. So in that sense, he supposed it amused him to have the *word* penis in his mouth. Was that what Malamar meant?

Malamar shook his head, glancing at his watch again. "Wah, f...uh...I have news for you, boys. This has only happened recently, but your parents knew about it, which is why they sent you here. The world has grown sick of *deviants* spreading the poison of AIDS through our society. The governments of Earth have been rounding up their homosexuals and exterminating them. At long last! Now," he boomed over a growing murmur, "each of your has AIDS in your blood; it is created when the homosexual urge is indulged. It preys on *weakness*, and you are all four-course meals. You are here so that we can fix you, and save you. Make you *strong*, strong enough to defeat the AIDS that's coursing through your veins. We must make you *Men*, or when you return home, the police will come for you. And they will deal with you accordingly."

Quazi elbowed Scott. *Told you*, he mouthed.

Back on stage, Malamar had given up on trying to hide his interest in his wristwear. "You are the final fags on the planet. Homosexuals. Everything that we do at First Stone, we are doing for *you*. You will realize the errors of your ways. You'll repent. And you'll *thank* us for having made you productive Men of the world, fit to spread the Word of God, and not the, uh, the AIDS of…Gay. And everyone said Amen."

No one said Amen.

"Everyone said Amen!"

Everyone said Amen.

His work done, Malamar turned on a heel and strode off the stage. Rowan took his place. As Malamar had taken the mic with him, the unhappy head counselor had no choice but to shout over the rising din.

"Everyone relax!" he cried. His mouth was a perfect downturned crescent, like that of a ventriloquist's dummy. "The disease will not kill you immediately. We are going to work with you, to save you from this scourge!"

Brobson was terrified by this announcement, as he had been by all of this evening's revelations. Not only was he gay; he had AIDS, and the government wanted to kill him. It was hard to believe…until he heard Rowan say it. *The disease will not kill you immediately. We are going to save you.* Malamar had said more words…but Rowan had said more.

He turned to Fred. "Did you know about all that?"

Shellshocked, Fred just stared at the mumbling Rowan on the stage. "No…they never said…"

Quazi trembled. Scott threw his arm around him. "I just went to the doctor two months ago," Quazi whimpered. "He said I was really healthy. Didn't say anything about AIDS."

"Maybe," Fred replied, "but he wasn't a Reverend Doctor. That's, like, twice as good, I bet."

Ned was looking down at his arms, perhaps trying to spot the disease's impression beneath his skin. He mouthed something to himself, but Brobson couldn't make out what it was.

Still and all, beneath the horror of his situation, a nugget of uncertainty rolled around in the basin of Brobson's braincase. The Reverend Dr. Keith Malamar had said that nobody was born gay…but Mom had told Brobson that he had been born in sin. And being gay was a sin. So if he *was* gay, didn't that mean he was *born* like that?

Once again, Brobson and his four buddies took a walk and had a talk, and Brobson was hardly present for either.

ELEVEN

CAMPFIRES WERE SUPPOSED to be fun. You sit around, sing some songs, maybe roast some marshmallows. Or weenies. There are all sorts of things you can impale on a stick and dangle over an open flame; the dangling is itself the point.

Nobody was dangling anything over the little flames scrabbling for purchase in the rock-and-stick pile. Those campers who hadn't already retired to their cabins sat on logs, rocks, and dirt, watching a primitive wonder and thinking only of the infernal realm it presaged. The Reverend Dr. Keith Malamar would be very surprised to hear that *none*, absolutely *zero*, not a *one* of these boys had dangling weenies on their mind.

Brobson sat on an atypically comfortable stone, head resting on his folded arms, themselves resting on his knees. He looked up, and in the flickering dreamlight he saw Fischer's face appear against the dark and vanish an instant later. Of course, it had never really been there. That was just the fire talking.

"That was something, huh?" the fire asked.

From the canvas of night, Hal painted himself into the scene. He sat down across from Brobson with a *flump.* "I only found out Keith was…sorry, the *Reverend Doctor,* was coming earlier today. Didn't say why. Now I guess we know." He picked up a stick and traced meaningless lines into the dirt.

"Is it true?" asked one of the kids Brobson hadn't properly met yet. "Do we all have AIDS?"

Quazi leaned forward, whispering like the cool guys in the movies. "Is the government killing all of the gay people?"

Hal continued carving his brand into the beaten flesh of their planet. His jaw juked from side to side; the poor guy was clearly overcome with the same fear. Perhaps he was also…?

"You know," he finally grumbled, eyes locked on the ground, "Rowan sure thinks so, but that was the first I've ever heard of it."

Not being a flat denial, that was clearly a confirmation. The kids all looked at each other as though they'd just discovered that Rowan Monteagle was a million spiders in a human suit; shocked, scared, but not surprised.

"So if we can't get fixed while we're here…" Ned trailed off.

Fred picked the thought up: "We're gonna get killed."

Panicked faces turned towards Hal, who could only look disapprovingly at what he'd drawn. "I'm afraid I *have* to say…yes." As the other boys fell into deep wells of despair, Brobson kept his gaze fixed on Hal. The junior counselor looked up at his sole remaining observer. And he looked…

Put it this way: in the past, when somebody told Brobson that something bad was going to happen to him because of his sinful ways, they'd looked pretty pleased about it. Not *obviously* so, it wasn't as though they were ready to jump up and click their heels together. It was more a *farted in an elevator and successfully avoided suspicion* kind of pleasure.

Hal didn't look like that. He just sat there with a stony frown on his face, a gargoyle with hemorrhoids.

All that night, Brobson dreamt about that face, suspended just beyond the luminance of the fire. Each time the wood popped, the light grew bolder for a moment – and as it reached towards Hal's face, it chipped off some of the detail. Slowly, Hal's face flaked and fell like scales from Saul's eyes.

Just before he woke up, the man without a face rose to his full height and stepped into the light. The wood popped one last time. Brobson saw that the man without a face was no man at all.

And then the fire was all there was.

TWELVE

OH, AND THE fire alarm.

It was a much more panicked alarm than Brobson was used to. The one in his house went *beep beep beep, beep beep beep*. This one howled, *aaurr-rrrrooooooooOOOOOOOOOO...*

Brobson opened his eyes. The alarm wasn't in his dreams. Was it? He cocked his head to the side and looked out the window. Clinging to the screen was a giant spider the size of his hand, with the fingers spread if you counted the legs.

"BLAAAAAUUUUUGGGGGGGHHHH," Brobson announced as he did the first sit-up of his life, hitting his head on the beam of the regrettably low cabin ceiling. "Ah!" He clapped his hand to his forehead, the hand that was the same size as the spider, this was how the spider would feel on his forehead! "Ghhhhlllll," Brobson finally concluded as he flipped out of his top bunk and, remarkably, stuck the landing.

He looked up. Everyone in the cabin was tucked comfortably into their sleeping bags (First Stone provided no bedding), oblivious to both the banshees at their door and the spider on Brobson's window.

"There's a big spider on my window!" he explained, hand rubbing his head.

A few kids with useful vantages turned their attention to Brobson's window, and confirmed his story by squealing and retching. The boy on the bunk below Brobson's leapt out of bed and joined Brobson in the center of the cabin.

For a while, they all looked at the spider. Then, cool as the inside of Brobson's insulated lunch box, Fred (who had the bunk below Scott – Ned and Quazi were in other cabins) rolled out of bed, grabbed a broom that was tucked between the far wall and one of the beds, and clambered onto Brobson's bunk.

"Be careful!" Brobson cried over the descending howl (*OOOOOOOOOOOOoooooooooooaaaaa...*), reminding himself of the most boring character in all of his favorite movies he wasn't supposed to have seen.

Those characters were usually women.

Fred wound up, took a practice swing, and smacked the unsuspecting arachnid right in the silk pouch. The spider curled its legs up and cannonballed into Brobson's bunk. Fred turned back to the rest of the boys and announced "all clear", certainly reminding himself of his favorite character in all of his favorite movies. The Manly character.

70

Just as the nightmarish howl outside began winding itself back up, the door swung open. Brobson turned, uneasy at how he would react to seeing Hal's face back in one piece. It was a question for which the answer would have to wait, as it was Rowan Monteagle whose silhouette stood in relief against the antiseptic blue of an ungodly hour.

Fred, who was positively bursting with courage this morning, made no attempt to lunge back into his bed as Brobson did (quite literally: Brobson dove headfirst into Fred's abandoned bunk). He stood ramrod straight, broom clutched at his side like a Staff Dad waiting for a new camper.

"What in God's good graces is transpiring here?" Rowan wondered.

From the top bunk, Scott played the role of cavalry: "Sir, a spider invaded Brobson's personal space, so Fred smote it with the broom."

Rowan pounded into the cabin, heavy boots warping the wood of the floor. "Who said you could do that?"

Without missing a beat, Scott told him. "Wherein the king granted the Jews which were in every city to gather themselves together, and to stand for their life, to destroy, to slay, and to cause to perish, all the power of the people and province that would assault them, both little ones and women, and to take the spoil of them for a prey. Esther chapter eight verse eleven, Sir."

Brobson looked up at the underside of Scott's mattress, marveling at the masterstroke. Rowan couldn't punish somebody for knowing the Bible *too well*. Could he? Brobson turned back to the head counselor to find out.

Rowan, face dropping right along with the unhappy siren, thought about Esther chapter eight verse eleven. "Well," he concluded, "we're not Jews." He harrumph-ed and walked out the door, the cabin moaning under each footfall. He left the door open in his wake, welcoming in the rising siren.

"Um," Brobson finally said to break the not-so-silence, "what's that noise?"

"Wake-up call," replied one of the boys whose names Brobson would never know.

Everyone shuffled out of bed, into their clothes, and out the door. Before following suit, Brobson crept up to his bunk, to take the corpse of the slain spider out with him and see about a proper burial.

He couldn't find it anywhere.

THIRTEEN

REAKFAST WAS, LIKE dinner, slop. This was vaguely brownish slop, presumably to put the unhappy customer in mind of pancakes and French toast and oatmeal. It did indeed conjure up thoughts of these foods, as well as provide a glimpse into how they must look halfway through the digestive tract.

After their balanced (on the lip of the uncanny valley) breakfast, they converged on the central pavilion. So concerned was Brobson about eight-legged intruders, he forgot all about that seven-letter word that had bedeviled him the evening prior: *ordeals*. So as Rowan and Hal broke all the campers up into groups, Brobson took the assertion that they were going hiking at face value.

BROBSON'S CALVES WERE on fire, and they weren't even halfway to wherever they were going. He was disappointed he was struggling so much, but it certainly made sense. It had been quite some time since Brobson had hiked. Well, he'd really only ever "hiked", which was to say he walked along dusty, negligibly sloping paths that amounted to God's handicap accessible ramp. They got you to less impressive lookouts, yeah, but the alternative was *hiking*, which entailed ropes and little clippy gizmos and sometimes reaching for your partner, who would be dangling by his fingertips, and shouting *grab my hand!* Which would be gay. It was weird that he was thinking about that, because he'd never had those sorts of thoughts before First Stone. Thoughts about how things could be gay. But, well, that's just an education, right? He was learning how the world worked.

Brobson pondered this, while the canopy above them grew thicker and the forest below them darker.

Some counselor Brobson hadn't encountered yet, who Quazi quietly identified as Louis, met them in the clearing and fanned the boys out into a large circle. Each of them was to be paired off with the boy directly across the circle from them. Naturally, Brobson and Quazi ensured that they were thusly positioned.

Louis announced the exercise, which sounded innocent enough: they were each to look at the boy across from them, and describe that boy.

A few other pairs went, but Brobson wasn't paying attention to what they said. He was listening to the hesitant way they said it, the way they smiled like they were trying to force their baby teeth out whenever Louis told them they did a good job. He saw it all, right there, in that moment. Everything Quazi had said was true. O-R-D-E-A-L-S, Amen. They could hurt the kids here, and the parents knew it. Not only that: they *allowed* it. They *paid* for it! All to have their kids fixed so the government wouldn't kill them. First Stone was here to put boys like Brobson all right, like a doctor resetting a dislocated shoulder. This will only hurt once, the parents must have figured.

To look at the other boys' faces, that didn't look like it was true.

Brobson described Quazi as "funny" and "smart". Louis told Brobson that he couldn't *see* either of those, so they didn't count. Brobson changed his answer to "has a nice smile", which Louis was not at all happy about, but accepted because there were some even unhappier clouds gathering on the horizon. Quazi described Brobson as "average height" and "soft", which Louis was fine with. That annoyed Brobson.

It rained before they could get back to their cabins.

BROBSON HADN'T BROUGHT boots with him, which was turning out to have been stupid. His sneakers were the cool one's he'd already wrecked once, and yet the mud still wanted them, *real* bad. Once or twice he was quite certain the muck had successfully wrenched his shoe from his foot. But much to his surprise, he'd done just a heck of a job on his laces.

On the way down, he asked Quazi why he'd described him as "soft". To this Quazi said "um, whoops" as he slipped on the mud, and then only wanted to talk about how slippery the mud was.

At some point, Brobson let slip that the circle format of that last exercise reminded him of this creepy dream he'd had last night. In conjunction with the spider, Quazi found this terribly exciting. "I'll tell you what that means tonight," he kept insisting. When Brobson recited variations on the theme of No Time Like The Present, the mud got even more slippery for poor Quazi.

In stark contrast to his feelings immediately upon waking, Brobson could now hardly wait for the evening to come. Evening, that was another seven-letter word that had less nightmarish connotations. Which was kind of funny, Brobson thought. Because evening is when nightmares come.

Of course, nightmares come in other seven-letter words, too.

FOURTEEN

"THERAPY," REPEATED THE happy grand-dad. He was kind of short, with a scooped posture that made him look like a question mark. That was as it should be. This Ancient dust man, who had introduced himself as Dr. Morzo and then pointed to a framed piece of printer paper on the wall and said "M.D." like he was taking issue with some-body who saw the glass as half full, asked even more questions than Dr. Lucas.

The difference, of course, was that Dr. Morzo also provided the answers.

"This is for your therapy." Dr. Morzo smiled softly. "You understand your predicament," his eyes snapped down to a paper on his desk and back up in record time, "Bronson?" The eyes went back down again, and Dr. Morzo gave his head a microscopic little shake.

77

"We need to make you well, or the government is going to kill you. It will not be nice for you, no? No."

Brobson squirmed in his chair. This small room was actually the basement of the nurse's office, accessed via a rust-spotted bulkhead. It was a very weird place to put a doctor's office, *much* weirder than the back of a church two counties over – maybe Dr. Morzo had built his office, with its dusty frames on the walls and unnervingly *un*-dusty punching bag slouched in the corner, and then the nurse tacked his place on as a second story, only it was so heavy the doctor's room sank down into the Earth?

Probably not, but in this new world where he had AIDS and the government wanted to kill him, Brobson felt ready to believe anything. Still, he didn't understand the purpose of this. But what else was new.

"I, uh, Sir…I don't un-"

Dr. Morzo grinned so warmly, Brobson expected to see beads of sweat spotting his forehead any second now. "You needn't call me Sir, son. Do you mind if I call you son? Of course not. It's not uncommon."

"Sure, th-"

"Son, do you understand that I'm here to help you?"

Brobson, caught off guard by being expected to actually answer a question, nodded.

"And do you understand that an unconventional therapy will be required to address your unconventional deviance?"

"Um, what does unconventional mean?"

Another treacly grin. "It means different, Br…son."

78

"Oh, uh…yeah. Sure. B-"

"Then why don't you engage with the exercise? Or do you not want to get better, Brobson? Brob*son?* May I call you Brob, son? Ha! Don't you want to get better?"

Brobson opened his mouth.

Dr. Morzo nodded. "Of course you do."

Brobson closed his mouth. Yes, that was more like it.

"*Now*, shall we begin again? I shall play the role of your father, and you will just be yourself." Dr. Morzo's smile flickered like a candle at a funeral.

That directive, 'be yourself', was only part of what baffled Brobson about this. Being himself was what had gotten him into this mess, cast him as a disease-riddled, prepubescent enemy of the state. Wasn't he here to be made *better* than himself?

"Son," boomed Dr. Morzo in a throaty baritone that indicated both that the exercise had resumed, and that Dr. Morzo had definitely never met Brobson's dad. "You had something you wanted to say to me? You did."

Yes, Brobson had something he wanted to say to him. It was what Dr. Morzo had told him he wanted to say. "Ah…yeah, Dad, I, um, I was…it made me un-happy when you didn't hang the drawing I made in Ms. Bauhoff's class on the fridge." That was a true story that Dr. Morzo had extracted via a prolonged, rather graceless interrogation. What wasn't true was that Brob-son would ever say "you b…better hang it up now."

"No," Dr. Morzo sighed, "I don't think I will, son. I

79

think I'm going to keep ignoring you, and keep neglecting you."

"Oh, ok."

Another sigh. "Don't you want to know why I'm neglecting you, and not providing you with a strong father figure?"

Brobson thought about it.

"It's because I can't love anyone other than your mother. We have no love left for you. How does that make you feel?"

There was no answer to that question because the premise didn't make sense. Brobson's parents had made a thing out of telling him they loved him even as they dropped him off here. And hadn't they put him in this camp because they loved him, and didn't want him to die? If they didn't love him, they'd have just let the government take him away.

"Oh, I can see, son. I can see it makes you angry." Dr. Morzo splayed out his fingers and tapped the tips together. "Just like I'm sure it makes you angry that I used to touch you when you were young. Do you remember it?"

What did he mean, touched? It wasn't clear, but what was clear was that the way Dr. Morzo was using that word was very, very wrong.

"How angry are you right now, son? You're very angry. Perhaps too angry to simply sit there and take my abuse any longer? Perhaps, it's likely. What are you going to *do* about it, son? Are you going to let me get away with this? How could you? You can't."

None of this made any sense, but the scary part was that it *did*. Brobson was getting angry, which wasn't an emotion he often felt. He didn't have a temper the way some other kids at school did. *Chill*, that was the word his classmates used to describe him when they were feeling nice. *Quiet* was what his teachers wrote on his report cards. It wasn't even that Brobson felt the urge to scream and shout and then sat on the feeling; he didn't have the feeling to begin with. Most things were a-OK with him.

So why was he getting angry? He couldn't begin to imagine, but Dr. Morzo could. He had a perfectly rational explanation for Brobson's anger, and he laid it out, step by step. What's more, he was Ancient, which meant he really knew his onions. 'Experience', that was what Dad had always said people get as they get older.

Dr. Morzo had the most experience of anybody Brobson had ever met. So if certain parts of Dr. Morzo's story didn't make sense to him, who was he to poke at those soft bits? It was a story that still mostly made sense – and much like the stories in the Bible, it came from an Ancient source.

For all of the holes Brobson found in the explanation, could he offer a rival account of why he felt these feelings? No, he could not. That must mean something.

"We'll stop there for today, son. You did a good job." Dr. Morzo shuffled the papers on his desk, and mumbled Brobson's name a few times.

That was a left turn. "Thanks, Dad?"

Dr. Morzo stopped shuffling and looked up. "Hm?"

"I said thanks, Dad."

"No, I'm not your dad anymore. I'm Dr. Morzo again."

"Oh."

"Just think about what we've talked about here today. Think about the things you told me."

"Oh, yeah."

"And son, also now I'm your dad again, son?"

The skin under Brobson's right eye twitched. "Huh?"

"Don't tell people about the things I've done to you. It would be bad if anybody knew."

"…"

"You can go play now, son."

"Dr. Morzo?"

"Yes?"

"No, I was just making sure."

"Go play, son."

Not knowing what else to do, Brobson went out to play, even though it was still raining.

FIFTEEN

SCOTT SHOOK HIS head. "Dr. Morzo says *everybody's* got a bad dad."

"I have a bad dad," Quazi told the wind-whipped screen of Fred's window. It not being lights out yet, the kids were free to gather in whatever cabin they chose. A few kids with something to prove were huddled together in the rain, but Brobson, Ned, Fred, Quazi and Scott opted to huddle in the drier climes of Fred's bunk. This, Brobson noted as he stared at the crouched figures lit by the cabin's single, unenthusiastic bulb, was very gay. And gay was bad. But here they were.

"Me too," Fred added.

Scott shook his head again, or rather, had never stopped shaking his head. "Not the way Dr. Morzo is saying. Wh-"

Now Ned set his head a-shakin'. "You don't know that."

83

"I've had two sessions with Dr. Morzo," Scott explained, head still shaking. "I think I kn-"

"No, I mean, you don't know how bad their dads are."

"That's fair," Fred noted.

"W…th…" Scott harrumphed. "I'm just saying."

After a few seconds, Scott and Ned had shaken their heads out. The boys listened to the rain and tried to figure out what it meant that Dr. Morzo thought the same things about their different dads.

Fred sat up a bit straighter. "Hey, did you ever find the spider?"

"No," Brobson frowned. "I checked this morning."

Quazi tilted his head upwards, as though catching a scent. "You guys have heard about how it's bad luck, right?"

Ned cocked his head to the side – Brobson wouldn't have been surprised to discover that Ned practiced different head positions in a mirror, to find the ones that utilized his hair the most. "What's bad luck?"

"Killing the spider, but not killing it right."

Fred slumped back down.

Scott shook his head.

"It *is*," Quazi insisted.

Ned turned around and walked backwards. "Who says it's bad luck, Quazi? Aside from you."

Quazi shrugged. "Lots of people."

Ned gave Brobson an encouraging look. "I've never heard that."

Brobson wasn't the one most in need to reassurance,

84

though: "I'm the one!" Fred kept mumbling. "I killed it!"

"Oh, calm down," Scott hissed. "Quazi just made that up."

Quazi took umbrage. "Did not!"

"Where'd you hear that, then?"

"It's a thing that everybody knows, like don't walk under an umbrella!"

Ned tapped Quazi on the shoulder. "I think you mean a ladder, right?"

"Yeah! A ladder!"

"Because there's also you're not supposed to open an umbrella inside or else you'll get struck by lightning."

"Exactly!" Quazi shouted. Scott rolled his eyes, so Quazi pointed a trembling finger at Brobson. "If I made it up, then why did Brobson have a bad dream, huh?"

Fred made the sound of a squeaky toy being slowly flattened beneath a steamroller. "I had a bad dream too." The trembly way he said it was hard for Brobson to square with his cucumber-cool first impression of...

Hang on – were cucumbers *actually* cool?

Scott folded his arms. "Lots of people have bad dreams lots of nights. Especially here."

"Lots of spiders get killed lots of nights," Ned quite reasonably pointed out.

"So spiders make nightmares now?"

Quazi bounced up to his knees, spoiling for the fight. "Of course they do! They're scary!"

Ned pouted his bottom lip out, the universal expression for *dude's got a point*.

"Th…y…d…" Scott babbled. He continued, "bl… sp…"

"But Brobson didn't have just *any* bad dream," Quazi recounted with a hunching of the shoulders and raising of the hands. This was another universal expression, one which presaged a Spooky Story. "He had a dream about…Finchley."

Fred gasped. Ned nodded.

"Who's Finchley?" Brobson asked.

Quazi closed his eyes, shook his head and tutted. "Aren't you guys from here?"

"I am," Brobson replied. "Well, um, not First Stone. But Pennsylvania, I mean."

The others volunteered that they, too, were from Pennsylvania. "Wah!" Fred marveled.

"Pennsylvania is a big state," Scott mumbled.

Quazi tutted again. "All of you are from Pennsylvania, and none of you know the Tale of Finchley Shivers?" He turned to Brobson. "That explains why you didn't recognize his mark in your dream,"

"Finchley Shivers," Scott repeated, rolling his head around his neck. "Did he change his name after he became a scary goblin monster? Or he just got lucky with that spooky name, I guess?"

"He's not a *goblin monster*," Fred snapped, with a turn to Quazi. "Is he?"

"Of course not," Quazi said with an unappreciative look towards Scott. "And it's not his real name, obviously. Nobody knows his real name."

86

Scott scoffed. "But I'm sure we know everything about his st-"

"SHUT UP," cried the cabin. Startled, Scott looked around. Some of the other boys were looking his way.

"I've heard of Finchley Shivers," one of them announced.

"Me too," said another.

Flummoxed by the outgroup support, Scott's obstinance began to thin and peel. He turned back to Quazi. "Sorry."

"No worries, man," replied a Quazi who seemed incapable of the temper flares of which he was clearly capable. Relishing his audience, Quazi scooted towards the edge of the bed, feet dangling over the low drop. He smiled mischievously. "I wish there were thunder and lightning to go along with this rain, *eh*?" Right on cue, a flash of lightning and a crack of thunder missed their cue. Quazi listened to the soothing softshoe of the rain, shrugged, and sourced a flashlight from one of the boys listening on the other end of the cabin. Naturally, he shined it at the bottom of his chin. "Can somebody turn out the light?" Somebody did.

Much to Brobson's embarrassment, he felt the hair on the back of his neck rising.

SIXTEEN

S O," QUAZI GRINNED, careful to show all of his teeth, "nobody really knows who Finchley Shivers was, or what his real name was. Somebody just started calling him Finchley Shivers at some point, and it stuck."

Scott inhaled sharply, and received an elbow in the ribs for it.

Quazi continued, "all we know is that he was a young kid…just about *our age*. One day he got sent into the woods by his parents to chop down a tree. In olden times, everything was made out of trees. This takes place in olden times, I forgot to say.

"Anyway, Finchley goes walking alone into the woods, and it's all foggy out and nighttime. He's looking for the best tree to cut down, but none of them are big enough, because the biggest tree would be best to cut down. Finally, he finally finds a great big tree. It's so

89

big it disappears into the smoke. Like, up above him. As Finchley's looking up at it though, he's smiling and then it starts to rain. Like, hard. Just like it's doing, right…*now*." Quazi gestured out the window, where it was hard to tell if it was still raining or if there were just droplets sliding off the leaves above them.

Ever undaunted by uncooperative environs, Quazi turned his attention back to the interior of the cabin. "He's pretty sure he wouldn't be able to find this tree again if he left now, because it was so dark and misty. But he also definitely has to get out of the rain or else he'll get sick and die because in olden times medicine hasn't been invented yet.

"So what he does is he crawls into this hole under the tree…" Quazi demonstrated by flopping to his feet and crouching beneath the bunk. "…like this little dirt cave so he's right underneath the tree, and the roots are dangling over like this…" He took stock of his available props, and then tugged the sleeping bag part way off of Fred's mattress pad. "…and now he can sleep here and be out of the rain, and he doesn't have to worry about not finding the tree again because he'll be sleeping under it the whole time."

"The tree runs away," one of the kids on the far end of the cabin predicted.

Another shook his head. "There's a witch in the cave."

"Could also be a bear," a third chimed in.

"This isn't a bear story!" the second kid hissed. "This is a witch story!" He turned back to Quazi. "Right?"

Quazi, hardly believing his luck, pressed on without answering. "So in the morning Finchley wakes up in the little cave, he stretches…" Quazi demonstrated by stretched his legs out from beneath the bunk. To do so, he leaned his head back, concealing it from their view.

And then he screeched like a teakettle.

All of the boys screamed, diving into their sleeping bags or covering their faces with pillows.

"What is it?" Brobson asked from behind the impenetrable barrier of his hands over his face.

"It's here!" Quazi cried. This was a genuine terror, none of his winking storyteller's voice. He scrambled out from under the bed, scooting back but never standing, which seemed a strange choice. "It's there!" He corrected himself with an outstretched finger.

Brobson flipped on the lights. Scott leapt down to the floor and wrapped Quazi in a gentle hug. "What is, man? What's there?"

"The spider!"

Ned leapt off of the bed to investigate, clambering down onto all fours. "Flashlight," he ordered as he opened his palm and turned it skywards.

"Flashlight," Scott echoed as he lay the instrument into the questing hand.

Ned shone the fearless beam under the bed, and crawled in after it. For a moment, all anyone in the cabin could see were his feet, shifting as he moved left and right. After at least a minute of this, his feet stopped and he said "Huh!"

"Whuh?" Fred demanded.

"It's Brobson's spider, alright!"

Brobson shook his head. "It's not *my* spider."

Ned reversed himself out from under the bed. "But what's it doing all the way over here? Fred killed it over there." He indicated where *there* was by pointing with a hand that clutched the fallen spider.

And there was a great hew and cry in cabin three.

When this subsided, aided by Fred flinging open the door and *demanding* that Ned ditch the bug, as well as Scott's obligatory reminder that spiders aren't *actually* bugs, all eyes in the cabin fell to Fred.

"How did it wind up there?" Ned wondered redundantly. "You killed it over *there*."

"Maybe it *knew* Fred killed it," one of the nameless brainboxes offered.

Scott debunked this immediately. "Spiders don't *know* anything."

"And besides," Ned added, "how would it get over there if it had been killed? In the first place?"

Sensing that this exchange could go on for quite some time, Brobson did something he'd never done before. He interrupted.

"Wait a second," he blurted out without even thinking about it, because if he had thought about it then of *course* he wouldn't have just blurted it out, that's *rude*, "I want to hear the end of Quazi's story. What happened to Finchley when he woke up?"

Quazi surveyed the room, which was now well lit and full of boys who were relieved that the spider was gone. He shrugged. "It's not gonna be good now."

Everyone made disappointed baboon noises.

"Nobody's scared anymore!" Quazi lay one palm flat, and chopped the other into it repeatedly. "The whole *point* is that you are *spooked* by the *story*. Nobody's spooked anymore."

"So spook us again!" Ned suggested, half-imploring and half-teasing.

"Yeah!" cried the chorus.

Quazi folded his arms. "That's not how spooking works. I set the mood with the lights and flashlights and it was really good. I'm never gonna be able to spook you that good again."

"Just tell us how it ends, then," Brobson said in his most conciliatory voice. And then, because old habits died hard, he added "please."

Quazi shook his head. "You're all gonna think it's dumb. It's really scary if you're spooked, but i-"

"Just tell us!" Scott demanded.

Fred did a small double take, and then agreed enthusiastically.

Quazi sighed. "Alright, so, Finchley wakes up and tries to stretch, but he can't because the hole he came in through is gone. The tree like, rearranged its roots in the night, and now Finchley is trapped in the dirt cave under the tree. So he starts trying to dig his way out, only no matter where he digs there's just more root. It's like he's in a little Christmas ornament of tree roots, except underground. And then the tree slowly sucks him in, and it, like, it kind of absorbs him. So he's now up in the trunk of the tree, like if the tree weren't there it

93

would look like he was just standing and hovering in the air, except in a tree. And he's still alive, and he can see and hear and feel everything, he just can't move or talk or scream. And because trees live forever, now Finchley lives forever like that. He's just stuck hanging there for the rest of time and he wants to scream or cry for help but he can't, he just has to wait there knowing that eventually somebody is going to come and chop him down, and he's gonna feel it when they do."

Several thoughtful seconds pass, at the end of which the boy who foresaw that the tree would run away turned in the first review. "That's dumb."

"Yeah," Fred concurred. "Like, he just turns into a tree?"

Quazi frowned. "It would have been so much better if you'd stayed spooked. Then there are all these cool details that will definitely give you nightmares."

"Like what?"

"Like he can feel termites crawling around inside him, or how it hurts when his leaves fall off in the fall."

Fred shrugged.

"I think it's creepy," Ned said. "That he's just stuck there."

Quazi nodded. "Thanks."

Warming to self-assertion, Brobson rejoined the conversation. "Wait, you said you remembered this story because of something in my dream? And then it was related to the spider somehow?"

"Hey!" Ned flicked Quazi on the neck. "You were right about the spider!"

94

Finally rising to his feet, Quazi playfully slapped Ned's hand away. "There's a version of the story where lightning strikes the Finchley tree, and he escapes, but now he's half man half tree. And he doesn't have any face or anything, it's just tree bark for his skin. And it's always peeling off and moving around."

"Half man half tree," Scott mumbled to himself, amused.

Brobson nodded. "That does sound like the guy I saw in my nightmare. Except he started as Hal. What does that mean?"

"Mhm," Quazi said. "Mhm."

"But what does that have to do with the spider?" Fred asked.

"Aaaah...oh, um, nothing I guess. But Brobson *did* have the nightmare."

"Yes," Brobson allowed, "I did."

With a *creeaaaaaakkkk* that Quazi probably would have loved to have had at his disposal during the story, the door to the cabin inched open. Hal poked his head in. "Back to your own cabins, fellas." He slid back out, leaving the door ajar.

"Can *I* tell a story next time?" Ned asked as he heaved himself to the floor. "I know a bunch of really creepy stories. I know at least three of that kind of story. I love being scared when its on purpose."

Quazi flicked Ned on the neck. "I was telling a story, that doesn't mean we're trading stories now."

"I'd like to hear more stories," Brobson lied. The truth was, silly as the story of the half man half tree had been…

"Me too!" one of the kids in the far corner said.

"See?" Ned exclaimed. "Everybody wants more stories. I'll tell the next one!"

Ned, Quazi and a few of the others said their good-byes and filed out of the cabin. Brobson smiled at nothing in particular. Everybody wants more stories when the lights are on.

SEVENTEEN

YOUR FATHER WOULD turn out the light, and then what? He would whisper something."

"He'd say 'goodnight', sometimes?"

"And then what? He would close the door."

"Yeah."

Dr. Morzo nodded and leaned back in his chair. It would be during a pause like this that Dr. Lucas would have written something down on his little yellow pad.

Brobson had never seen Dr. Morzo write anything down.

"Son, if this is too hard to talk about…"

Brobson tilted his head like a dog at a gramophone. "No? It's just bedtime stuff."

Dr. Morzo's eyes flashed. "Is that what he called it?"

"Called what?"

"You can tell me, Son. I am a doctor." Another

gesture to his very favorite piece of decoration, that framed 'diploma'. "It'll be strictly between the two of us."

Brobson stared at his feet, hoping he could find some new detail he hadn't already gone over a million times. This was how the sessions with Dr. Morzo always went. Morzo asked questions, answered his own questions, and then stared at Brobson, who would in turn stare at his shoes because what the heck was Dr. Morzo talking about?

He kept telling Brobson that Dad had touched him. Which, like, duh? Dad would pick him up on his shoulders to watch the parade go past, or hold him above water as he taught him to swim. Dads always touched their sons, because everybody touched everybody. Didn't people who found religion even say God touched them? What, did Dr. Morzo go around never touching anybody?

But there was that way he used the word *touch*, though. Like it had something inside it that wasn't sweet, but sour.

"What did your father do after he closed the door? He came to your bed, and shook you awake."

Brobson frowned at his shoes. "I don't know what he did after he closed the door beca-"

"Because why? Because he would cover your head with a pillow!" Dr. Morzo sounded *very* excited at the prospect.

"No, because he would go downstairs and watch an adult movie."

"Movies about men and boys. "

"Maybe. They were movies little kids aren't supposed to watch."

"And he made you watch them? He did."

"No, he never let me. He once told me he would show me manly adult movies when Mom wasn't home, but never did."

Dr. Morzo nodded like he was trying to dislodge a toupee. "Like what? They had titles like *Head of the Firm 4.*"

Brobson shrugged. "I forgot most of them. *Predator,* he talked about a lot. *Die Hard. Jack Reacher.*"

Dr. Morzo's mouth flatlined. He paused, thought, and then rummaged through the papers on his desk until he found a pen. *"Hard Predator? Jackin' Reach Around?"*

"Jack Reacher."

Dr. Morzo wrote this down – though he seemed to be writing just a bit longer than those two words would necessitate – then clicked his pen and smiled at Brobson. "Go and play."

EIGHTEEN

H OW'S THIS?" NED asked as he positioned the flashlight beneath his chin.

"Bring it forward like an inch," Quazi said.

Ned brought it forward like an inch. "Now?"

Quazi shot him a thumbs up.

Ned slowly raked his eyes across the darkened cabin, now far more populous than when Quazi had held court. Word had spread that there was a good spook story to be found in cabin three…for those who had courage.

"Ok," began Ned's terrifying tale, "one time there was this family that took a vacation that worked out really bad for them." What followed was, Brobson would eventually discover, a broadly accurate synopsis of *The Shining*, which Ned had read over the course of two months at his friend Polly's house. Polly had an allowance, and used it to buy paperbacks her parents

101

would totally kill her if they found out she had. Ned and Polly would often do their homework during recess, tell their parents they were working on it together at home, then just sit and read. It was, according to Ned, "really fun".

Ned, pleased as all get out that nobody else had read *The Shining*, finished by saying "and then that's the end."

He clicked off the flashlight, and the boys all squealed. A moment later, Fred flipped the ceiling light on, illuminating their laughter.

"But what still happens?" one of the boys asked.

Ned blinked. "In the story?"

"Yeah," Quazi said, "that's a good question. In all good spook stories, there's something that still happens to this day. Like *they say if you listen close, you can still hear the lady crying behind a bush* or something."

The first boy placed his arms sagaciously upon his knees. "That's right. They're not supposed to just end, they're supposed to go on forever."

Ned scratched behind his neck. "Um…well, uh, I guess if you go back to the hotel you can still hear the Bad Dad just whaling on himself with a giant wooden golf club thing?"

Brobson rolled onto his back, and then flipped back to his butt. "So wait, what happened to the Bad Dad?"

"He died when the boiler exploded," Scott was delighted to remind them.

Ned nodded. "The boiler is a symbolism."

Fred cocked his eyebrow. "Wouldn't that make it hard to go back to the hotel to hear the Bad Dad's ghost? If the hotel blew up?"

"Maybe," Ned granted.

Scott leaned forward. "Boilers can explode, and also wasps are real. But ghosts aren't real and plants don't move."

Brobson furrowed his brow. "Except for the Holy Ghost."

"Well yeah, obviously."

Quazi tapped his chin theatrically. "But there were moving plants in my story, and also in Ned's…so maybe plants *do* move? Just when you're not looking! Oooooh!" He waved his hands at Scott, who rolled his eyes, as was his wont.

There followed a discussion about ambulatory plants that Brobson tuned out. The Bad Dad *had* died, hadn't he? It wasn't often that Brobson heard stories where Moms and Dads died, and their death was a good thing. Usually it was a very sad thing, or else the Moms and Dads just lived forever.

But they could die, and you didn't always have to be sad about it. He knew that he would be sad if his parents died, because he loved them. But, still, the idea that he would be sad for a *reason*, and not because he *had* to be…

Wild.

NINETEEN

DR. MORZO PUT two patches on Brobson's hands, one on the left and one on the right. They were each white, about the size of a postage stamp. Dr. Morzo stuck them to the meat between Brobson's thumb and pointer finger. Wires ran from them, snaking around the table before finally getting their act together and making a beeline for Dr. Morzo's little machine.

"So I've been ruminating upon what you told me a few days ago," he said as he fiddled with various knobs and spinners. "And I thought we'd try another little exercise to help you conquer your past traumas. How does that sound? It's a very good exercise."

Brobson grunted. It seemed a little strange for Morzo to be asking him what he thought about this new "exercise" after he'd already been wiped down and hooked up for it, but he also wouldn't have been surprised if that little piece of paper to which Dr. Morzo was so fond of pointing said "A Little Bit Strange" under the man's name.

Which, come to think of it, Brobson didn't actually *know* what it said. Actually.

Dr. Morzo nodded; in his line of work, a grunt was assent. He pressed a button on his machine, to which the machine said *bbbooooooOOOOP!*

"I'm going to show you some things, and you're just going to look at them. It's that simple. Doesn't that sound simple? It really is that simple." He flipped a switch. *SCREEEEEEEE*, the machine elaborated.

Little Bit Strange, MD flipped around his laptop so the screen was facing Brobson. The words "AVERSION S15 LUTZ" on a dull white background confronted him for a moment, and then vanished as Dr. Morzo reached around the monitor and pecked the space bar.

What replaced the text was a picture that had probably been taken from the catalogue of a store Brobson's parents couldn't afford to buy things at. It was a Man and a woman, both white, the Man slender but with well-defined, sunbaked musculature atop a navy blue pair of bathing trunks, his hair short on the sides and long on top, flopped to the right (Brobson's right, so the Man's left) in a stylish but playful manner.

The woman had on a bikini, and her boobs were so big Brobson couldn't understand how she could put on a seatbelt.

"Who jumps out at you more?" Dr. Morzo asked.

And then, miracle of miracles, he *didn't* immediately provide the answer.

Brobson decided to answer honestly. He said it was the guy. Big mistake.

Like a whip-crack in slow motion, the patch on Brobson's right hand shot fire through his entire arm. Tears sprang into his eyes before his mouth had a chance to vocalize his agony.

"Look at the picture, son!" Dr. Morzo shouted over Brobson's scream. "Look at the man to whom your degeneracy draws you!"

The pain intensified. Brobson scratched at the patch with his left hand. Dr. Morzo shot his own hand out, catching Brobson's left wrist and squeezing hard as the inferno in his right hand raged.

Brobson raised his eyes to Dr. Morzo, and saw something more terrifying than any of the stories he'd heard in cabin three.

He saw *nothing*.

"Look at it, son," Dr. Morzo demanded. "If you don't look at it, I'll only make the pain worse. This is for your own good."

Brobson flailed his right hand, which Dr. Morzo immediately caught with his free hand. Unable to do anything else, he tried to blink the tears out of his eyes as his feet tapped out a miserable rhythm on the floor of the basement. "I don't get it!" he cried. "You're hurting me!"

"I'm trying to save your life!" Dr. Morzo screamed.

He hit another button. The fire in Brobson's hand

burnt itself out, but still the embers smoldered. Morzo let go of Brobson's wrists, never taking his empty eyes from the face of the boy he was trying to save.

Without a word, Dr. Morzo hit the space bar on the computer again. This time the image that appeared was of a Man with preposterous muscles, glazed like a donut. He was wearing just enough fabric to cover his sinful bits, and that laughable little tissue was clearly working overtime.

A sheet of ice pierced Brobson's left hand. This time, Dr. Morzo reached out and clamped his wretched meathooks over Brobson's wrists immediately.

"Look at it!" he hollered over Brobson's wailing. "Look at the picture or your government is going to hunt you down and kill you! I AM THE ONLY ONE WHO CARES! ARE YOU TRULY THIS UN-GRATEFUL?!"

Brobson was, apparently, this ungrateful. He tried as hard as he could to look at the picture, but couldn't stop blinking, trying to clear his vision so he could look at the d...the dang...the *damn picture!*

But he couldn't do it. He couldn't look at it. And so Dr. Morzo was true to his word – he made the pain so much worse.

TWENTY

IT SEEMED STUPID now. They were descending towards the mess hall, sparring over who would get to tell the spooky story that night. One kid thought his would really scare the pants off of everybody, but another had one that was pretty gross, which was kind of like scary but better. Shocking as any he-was-dead-all-along twist, the wet blanket known as Scott volunteered *himself* as spooky storyteller. This tease proved irresistible, and he was quickly granted the privilege by unanimous consent.

But why did it matter? Why were they sitting in the dark, holding a flashlight at an impractical angle and telling stories that they always said were true but were really (probably) made up? Why weren't they talking about how they were being hurt? Quazi had said the word, and perhaps that was enough for him. Was this their way of dealing with it? Pretending it wasn't happening? Reducing it to seven euphemistic letters?

How much went on at First Stone that nobody ever talked about? And why did that make Brobson feel *less* inclined to be the one breaking the silence?

SCOTT'S STORY, MUCH to everyone's surprise, was *very* creepy. The boy said he didn't believe in ghosts, but he sure knew how to play to those who did. It was about a guy who went camping in the woods (natch), and then a bunch of super creepy stuff happened.

"The thing about ghosts that everybody knows," Scott digressed part way through his tale, "is that they love to be creepy a little bit at a time. Exponentially, is what that's called. First they'll pile up a bunch of rocks and sticks outside your tent, very much like the pile of rocks and sticks *right out there*, and then maybe they'll rattle the trees and snap sticks, just like…" Scott paused, ear cocked theatrically to the window, "…just like *that*," he concluded, despite the distinct lack of both rattling eaves and crackling twigs. It was a testament to Scott's yarn-spinning prowess that Brobson *heard* the rattling and the snapping, even though he *knew* that neither had occurred.

"And then," Scott concluded, "once they've really creeped you out, that's when they get you."

At that point he resumed his story, which did indeed feature a ghost that teased out a gentle gradient of terror upon the hero. This climaxed on a dreary, moonless night. The protagonist, which each of the

110

boys imagined to be themselves (Scott was *very* good at this), awoke to hear someone scrambling around the darkness, right outside his tent. In his own mind, each boy slowly unzipped the flap of the tent, and came face to not-so-face with a pair of old, knobbly, naked knees. Scrambling backwards, each boy looked up, into the face of the world's weariest geezer. The oldtimer's face was buried beneath a massive white beard, the only part of his body with any, well, body. The rest of him looked like a skeleton in a grey jumpsuit two sizes too large.

"Help me," Scott croaked through this conjured horror, "they're coming, but they'll never get here. Help me."

With that, the old man ran out of the light and into the gloom of each boy's subconscious, where he could *really* do some damage.

Brobson had a feeling he'd be having a nightmare tonight, but Scott wasn't done – the next morning, the hero has a heck of a time finding his way out of the woods. He quickly realizes he's lost, and he just starts wandering, hoping to find an escape. He wanders for a week before he realizes that actually now *he* is a ghost, and he'd died a few days earlier. And now the ghost has just been wandering around the woods, and it gets older because in this story ghosts age even though in most stories they *don't*, and then of course he gets a big beard and he jumps out of a bush one night and finds a camp, so he starts wandering around until the camper opens the tent and it's HIM when he was younger! He was the old ghost that he saw!

"And he's still wandering the woods to this day," Scott concluded dutifully. "Trying to find his way out."

Brobson marveled at this story – in it, Scott placed them in the role of the hero, and took them to a world beyond death. And yet here they were, still in the cabin. They were all fine, and safe. Kind of. But whether or not ghosts existed, Scott's story brought something home to Brobson quite dramatically: one day he would get old.

He'd always known that he would die – his parents were so excited about Heaven, it was all they could talk about. It sometimes seemed like they could hardly *wait* to bite the big one, to such an extent that Brobson gave Mom some hard side-eye whenever she walked him just a little too close to the curb. So death was never far from his mind, as seemed to be the case with all good Christians.

What had always felt as fantastical and surreal as a song sung by a vegetable was the idea that Brobson would get *old*. One day he would be a scraggly geezer with a great big beard. In a way, thanks to the story, he already had been.

"Why don't we ever talk about how they're hurting us?"

Brobson tracked his eyes across the room, eager to leap up and hug whichever courageous soul had finally pointed out that the elephant in the room had no clothes. Seeing that everyone was looking intently at *him*, he deduced that *he* had been the courageous soul. He wondered if it counted as courage if he'd done it

112

without intending to.

He wondered if the room full of staring boys could even tell.

"I told you they did," Quazi mumbled. "We all told you."

Brobson nodded. "Telling and talking aren't the same, though."

"They electrocuted me," Scott offered without a pause.

Everyone hung their heads in a way that all but said *me too.*

Ned touched Scott's cheek, then pulled back in a way that would have made Dr. Morzo quite happy. "They only put these little things on me. They got hot and cold."

Brobson nodded. "I've had that one too."

"I've had both," Fred said in a voice more chilling than anything heard in any story. "The electrocution is way, way worse."

"I got the belt," a kid from the other end of the cabin added.

"I had that one," Quazi said.

"Which one?"

Quazi's eyes trembled, but his voice was forceful. "Elimelech."

The kid laughed without smiling. "I got Buzz. I don't know how you can remember the name of yours."

Quazi smiled without mirth. "I'll never forget it." Sensing confusion amongst the lucky, he explained: "Rowan's got a bunch of belts he keeps just for whupping kids, and he has a name for all of 'em."

"How do you know?" Scott asked, without a hint of his usual truculence.

The smile grew wider, the pits of his eyes deeper. "He tells you." He leaned his head back and closed his eyes. "I knew it. I knew it. My parents signed a piece of paper, and so Rowan whupped me." He lifted up his shirt and turned, wincing as he did, to reveal a thunderhead welt on his back.

Brobson felt like a fool for whining about his hot and cold treatment. He said as much. Quazi just shook his head and covered up the bruise. "It all hurts, man."

And suddenly Brobson felt a *hopeless* fool. They were all being hurt by adults, and their parents had agreed to it. So what could they do? Who could they tell? How could they make it stop?

Causing Brobson to wonder if maybe he had lost the ability to distinguish thoughts from speech, Fred answered his question. "We can't make it stop. They're not going to stop until we all be straight."

Quazi shuffled in his seat. "But that's good, right?" Brobson could hardly believe Quazi was defending the man who had lashed him with leather (that he'd seen fit to name!). But hardly believing was still the same thing as believing, in the end. "If they didn't do this," Quazi continued, "then we'd be gay forever. And then the government would kill us, so we couldn't spread AIDS. I'd rather get whupped with a belt than killed."

"I just don't see why I have to be not gay," Ned mumbled. "Nobody even knew I was gay until I told

114

them. So what if I'd never told them? They'd never know!"

"You'd still have AIDS," Quazi informed his hands.

"I didn't tell anybody," Brobson countered. "They told me."

"Same," Fred declared. "And I'll be honest, I never felt like I had AIDS in my blood until they told me."

Quazi shrugged at the floor. "What does AIDS feel like, though?"

Ned conceded the point on behalf of all of them with a slanting of the shoulders. "Just sucks. I don't get it."

"Neither do I," Scott practically whispered.

"...so what do we do?" Brobson asked.

Outside, branches rattled and twigs snapped. Nobody noticed.

TWENTY-ONE

AYBE DR. MORZO'S ears had been ringing. Brobson threw open the bulkhead behind the nurse's cabin and descended into
his regularly scheduled "therapy" session, only to be
met by the most solicitous iteration of his tormentor.
Had he *known* the boys had been talking about him?

Brobson and the doc chatted for a bit, Morzo con-
tinuing his tried and tired Dad schtick. Only this time
he introduced a new element.

"Do you recognize him?" Dr. Morzo asked as a man
who had probably been one of the Staff Dads emerged
from a gloomier part of the basement and sat at Morzo's desk.

"No," Brobson replied.

The man, it turned out, was here to roleplay Brobson's Old Father. Old Father and Dr. Morzo, the man
who would be New Father, launched into a little play
the latter had no doubt written. Old Father despised

New Father's masculine influences on his son. New Father cursed Old Father for corrupting the boy. Old Father rose to standing. New Father snapped up faster, grabbing Old Father and throwing him to the floor, right at Brobson's feet.

Then came the interactive bit.

As the cowering Old Father pushed himself up, Dr. Morzo grabbed the lumpy punching bag that had been raising questions in the corner and threw it down right where Old Father had been so recently trembling.

Old Father walked to the other side of the bag and stared down his Make Believe Son, shifting his weight from one foot to the other.

"I love you, son" whispered Dr. Morzo, the self-styled New Father. "I care about you." He took Brobson's hands in his own, gentle as could be, and peeled open the boy's fists. "But the time has come for you to be a Man." Into those supple palms, he lay a scuffed aluminum baseball bat.

Dr. Morzo pointed to the punching bag on the ground. "That is your Old Father, there. He is the one who has diluted your Masculine essence. What is to be your response to his feminizing influence?"

Brobson knew what the answer was – he was to take the bat, and thwack it into the punching bag that they were pretending was the Man who was pretending to be his father. But since everybody else was playing a stupid part, he figured he might as well too. So he shrugged his shoulders. "I dunno."

Smiling indulgently, Dr. Morzo told Brobson to take

the bat and thwack it into the bag, just in a lot more words.

Brobson stepped forward, grip tightening on the tape-wrapped haft of the bat, feeling the well-worried ends of those ancient strips shifting beneath his fingers. He studied the bag, and the Man it aspired to be, and only then fully appreciated how insane the session had become.

Until this moment, as he was hefting the bat over his head, feeling the muscles in his back moving in a way they never really had before, intuitively shifting one foot forward to maximize the power of his swing, everything had seemed par for the course. Even now, they weren't technically hurting him. Then again, maybe he'd just been defining the concept too narrowly.

Something had snuck through Brobson's defenses. It hurt more than all of Dr. Morzo's machines combined. Had Dad, his *Real* Dad, whose analog's analog he was preparing to clobber with a bat, known that this would be a part of the therapy and *agreed* to it? Had Mom? What were they trying to tell him? Did they *want* him to disown himself in this way, and hew to a New Father? Were they abandoning him?

Why wouldn't they?

He stared at the bag, trying to sculpt its plump indifference into something resembling his father. Oh, if only his imagination weren't so powerful. There, cowering before him, was his Real Father. And here he stood, bat raised, bones humming in anticipation.

And there he continued to stand.

"Be a Man, son!" Dr. Morzo screamed. "Do it! I can never be your New Father while the Old remains!"

It was almost enough to make Brobson smile, the absurdity of Morzo thinking that would in any way motivate him to swing the bat.

Something else that almost-but-didn't make him smile: the story about the Bad Dad who died in the hotel, and nobody was sad about it. If Dr. Morzo truly wanted to be Brobson's New Father, well…

Brobson goosed his imagination just a little bit more.

The bat came down fast, and the bag didn't have anything to say about it other than an anticlimactic *whunf* and a few wisps of well-hidden dust.

And yet, Brobson heard himself sob. Once, loud, hitching.

"Again," Dr. Morzo said. "Hi-"

Brobson didn't need to be asked a second time. His heart hurt, but it also felt good. Those sensations, pain and pleasure, grew stronger in both directions as he swung the bat again, and again, and again.

"AGAIN!" Dr. Morzo shouted over Brobson's man(l)y little deaths. "BE A MAN, BROBSON! GOOD! AGAIN!"

Sweat and tears burned his eyes and he swung the bat again. He cried his throat to shreds and he swung the bat again. His hands blistered and peeled and he swung the bat again.

So this was it. This was what it meant to be a Man. How wrong Brobson had been, how foolish. This was it. He swung the bat again.

TWENTY-TWO

NED PASSED THE salt, but he didn't look happy about it.

Brobson snatched the shaker out of his hand, taunted his grey slop with it, and plonked it back on the table.

The boys ate in silence for a full two minutes.

Finally, Ned rounded on Brobson. "What's your problem, dude? You're the calm friend."

Brobson cocked his head. "What's that supposed to mean?"

"Every group of friends has, like, *types*. Friend types. Scott's the jerk friend, and you're the calm one."

Scott paused, head hunched, spoonful of slop halfway towards his mouth.

Quazi patted him on the shoulder. "You *are* the jerk friend."

Spoon still aloft, head still lowered, Scott asked "which one are you?"

"I'm the rebel."

"Um," Fred interjected, "I don't th-"

Ned sighed. "Can we all like, let's just all agree that Brobson was the calm one."

Everyone just like all agreed.

"So?" Brobson snapped, knowing full well what Ned was getting at.

"*So*, why are you being a jerk?"

"Yeah, that's *my* thing!" Scott snapped, genuinely defensive.

Brobson folded his arms. "I'm *not* being a jerk." What was most annoying about this was that Brobson knew that he *had* been a jerk when he'd growled "gimme the salt" at Ned, when Ned had been in the middle of a story. Brobson also knew that he was being a jerk now. And he didn't like it. But his body was just sort of… doing it, without consulting him.

Ned turned to his audience. "He's being a jerk, right?"

Once again, they found themselves in agreement.

"Everybody knows you're being a jerk. So why?" His tone softened. "Are you good?"

Well, what a question that was.

Not knowing how else to answer, Brobson hung his head and confessed: "I beat up a punching bag with a baseball bat."

Quazi scratched the tip of his nose. "You're supposed to punch them, though."

122

Fred *hmmm*ed sagaciously. "They made you do that Old Father/New Father thing?"

Brobson nodded. "It was dumb. I knew it was dumb. I pretended it was Dr. Morzo I was hitting, b-"

"Wait," Scott cut in, "what is this?" He looked at Ned, who shrugged. Brobson explained his experience briefly, with Fred chiming in on minor points of divergence. For the most part though, their ordeals of the bag were largely identical.

"Point is," Brobson resumed, "I pretended it was Dr. Morzo who was the bag, and then I hit it and it made me kind of...happy. But not *happy* happy. It was like...I don't know. Like my heart was sick, and every time I hit the bag, I got a little bit of medicine. It felt good...*really* good. But it still felt bad. And now I just feel awful. I don't want to be a Man."

"What I don't get," Ned said after a healthy, thoughtful pause, "is that not every Man who's walking around the planet did this, right? So it can't be like just hitting a bag with a bat makes you a Man, because not everybody did that, right? There must be other Man things to do. Just, you know," he added as he took his spoon and slopped his alleged dinner around his plate, "not here."

"I've been thinking about leaving," Brobson was surprised to learn from his own voice. Had he? This was the first he'd heard about it. Once again, his body was just doing whatever it pleased without giving him a heads up.

Scott's head slid back like the band of a slingshot. He fired a hard little pellet at Brobson: "Don't."

123

Quazi looked at Scott, shocked. "Why not?"

"Because," Scott replied, savoring the opportunity to patronize, "we're really far from any place, that's the first thing. The second thing is the rule of threes."

Ned furrowed his brow. "What was the second thing?"

"This is the second thing. The rule of threes. I learned it on a TV show." Scott raised three fingers. "It goes…" the fingers dipped slightly. "Um…"

"Is this the one w-"

"Ah! Oh yeah!" Scott's digits regained their full height, only to drop one by one as a new rule emerged. "You can live for three hours without shelter, you can live for three days without water, and you can live for three weeks without food."

Quazi's mouth fell open. "Three *weeks?* Why would you wanna do that?"

"You don't do it because you *want* to, you do it because you *have* to."

Brobson forced a smile. "Well," he said with a nod towards his plate, "we've already gone almost three weeks without food."

The boys all laughed. It was one of the greatest moments of Brobson's entire life.

Ned was first to regain his composure. "Three hours without shelter? That can't be right. I've been outside for way longer than three hours."

"I bet he means sleeping," Quazi guessed.

Scott nodded. "I do."

"So," Brobson ventured, "couldn't we just leave and

not sleep until we get to shelter?"

"I once stayed up all night," Fred recounted. "Then my Stepdad asked me if I wanted pancakes and I fell asleep."

"I tried once," Ned added. "I wanted to play video games all night so I did, and then in the morning I had school and it was the worst day of school I ever had, and I've had a lot of worst days."

Brobson, before his body had turned mutinous, had always trusted his sense of sleepiness enough to never gainsay it. Running through the woods all day and night until he found safety was a cool idea, but in reality he almost certainly wouldn't manage it. No, he would have to sleep. So he would need to be able to find shelter.

...how long had his brain been thinking about this without looping him in?

"Anyway," Ned continued, "I was watching the trees on the way up. We are a *really* far ways away from everything."

"Like I said," Scott reminded everyone.

"I don't know if you could even run out of here in like two days, even if you didn't sleep. But if you didn't sleep you probably wouldn't be able to run for that long anyway."

"But if it takes longer," Quazi wondered, "how would you find food?"

"Hunt," Fred enlightened him.

Scott shot Fred the look he usually reserved for Quazi. "How?"

Fred shrugged. "Bow and arrow? Not my problem.

125

I'm not running away."

"I'm not either," Brobson said defensively. "I'm just saying, I was thinking about it."

Fred shrugged again, even more so. "I'm not even thinking about it."

Quazi put his silverware down and leaned forward, looking as excited by this illicit conversation as Brobson. "Why not?"

"If you get away, where will you go?" Fred waved his hands dismissively. "Your parents can just get you back."

Scott nodded in agreement. "They can send the police after you."

"Uh huh," Fred allowed. "My Mom and Dad got divorced, wh-"

"That's not Christian," Brobson dutifully observed.

"Uh huh. But they did, and then they were arguing over who I would live with. I had to live with my Dad, but I wanted to live with my Mom, so one day I just ran over to my Mom's house. Then the police came, knocked down the door, and took me back to my Dad's because he has the Custodies."

Ned blinked. "Woah! They knocked down your door?"

"Uh huh. I put up a fight but they got four of them to carry me away. I punched one of them, and he said it was the hardest punch he'd ever had."

"Gosh."

Now it was Scott's turn to say "uh huh".

Brobson puzzled over this dilemma. Where could he

go that his parents couldn't get him back? "What if they didn't know where I was?"

"They can still find you," Ned jumped in: he knew the answer from Polly's novels. "They have these machines that can find you by your hair, or if you spit on the ground they could analyze it and discover you. Also your skin and blood."

"Dangit," Brobson mumbled. That was almost all of the body parts. This was hopeless.

Not that it mattered, right? Running away wasn't an option. He would die in the woods, but even if he got home he would get his door kicked down by the cops. Also: what door? Where would he go? He had a really cool aunt in Phoenixville, Aunt Matilda, but he didn't know how to get there. He only knew that if you opened your left hand and turned it on its side so your four fingers were pointing to the right with your palm facing you, that sort of looks like Pennsylvania. And Phoenixville was down *there*, near the bottom right, where he had a freckle on his left pinky. There probably wouldn't be many markers in the woods leading to Pinky Freckle. No, he wouldn't be running away.

But he had no intention of returning to Dr. Morzo's basement. He couldn't face that punching bag again. He couldn't let it make him feel…that way. The scary kind of happy, the one that didn't make you smile.

He couldn't go, but he couldn't stay.

So what, then?

Lost in thought, he accidentally put some of the mess hall slop in his mouth and swallowed it.

TWENTY-THREE

BROBSON AND CO. were coming back from one of those aimless-yet-obligatory strolls through the woods, when Hal approached the cortege looking...lost, as though he'd just seen a ghost that had presented convincing evidence as to why ghosts can't possibly exist. He said something to the counselor leading the group, then slowed to a halt and waited for the procession to bring Brobson to him. Never had Brobson felt inevitability as palpably as he did approaching Hal just then.

"You have to come with me," Hal whispered when Brobson entered whisper-distance.

It wasn't a happy whisper.

Hal and Brobson broke off from the group. The latter shot an *I don't know* face back to his friends, who looked at each other and said things he couldn't hear. He was already out of whisper-distance.

HAL LED BROBSON to a golf cart parked on the gravel roundabout. Only half-joking, Brobson asked if he could drive it. Hal didn't say anything to that. Bad news.

They puttered back towards the entrance of the compound, the way Hal's parents had driven him in so many aeons ago. There loomed what looked to be the only building at First Stone with indoor plumbing, a great big wooden cabin with a handsome covered porch and a perfect brick chimney belching perfect silver smoke. It was a building built for a brochure.

Still without speaking, Hal lead Brobson up the steps to the porch, the boards of which were eerily silent beneath his feet.

Hal ushered Brobson through the door and into an office that, by the gargantuan taxidermy bird hanging from the ceiling, Brobson could intuit belonged to Rowan Monteagle. A *ker-snick* from over his shoulder told him that Hal had closed the door. He hoped against hope that Hal was still on *this* side of that perfectly set entry. He didn't have to turn around to know that he wasn't.

What Brobson faced, alone, was the eagle above and a bearskin rug below. On the wall to his right, a fire raged in an ornate fireplace. To his left, a window-mounted air conditioning unit blasted cold air into the room. In the middle of all this was Rowan Monteagle. He sat behind his desk, back as straight as he wished all young boys could be, hands laying spread on his desk, palms down. He looked like somebody had taken the batteries out.

As if hearing that thought, Rowan jolted awake. "I don't know how to speak to children," he growled.

Brobson stood exactly where he was, uncertain of what this was about but knowing perfectly well it wasn't good.

Rowan sighed, but somehow did it without moving his shoulders. "I don't quite understand the limits of your cognition and comprehension. Do you understand those two words?"

Brobson meant to reply with *No, Sir*, but found his lips had developed a sudden affinity for one another and simply could not be pried apart. So he shook his head.

Rowan nodded. "So we begin to chart the boundaries," he noted with neither malice nor compassion. "I delegate the task of interfacing with the children to others, as much as possible. My strengths are bureaucratic. How many of those words did you not understand?"

Brobson raised three fingers.

Without warning, God raised the volume. "ARE YOU MUTE, BOY?" Rowan bellowed this, and yet his posture remained exactly the same. Certainly not relaxed, but still...Brobson didn't think a person should be able to muster up such a guttural yell without at least frowning a little bit.

"N...no, Sir. I didn't understand three words. Sir."

"Yes," Rowan resumed at his previous volume, "and I expect I know which three. Hm. I've been informed that my disciplinary sessions can sometimes be...coun-

131

terproductive, as the boy up for reprimand may not wholly grasp the nature of their transgression. My goal here is productive. I aim to produce Men. I aim to provide clarity. What you boys lack is the latter, which frustrates your becoming the former. Therefore, I am, in my turn, frustrated to learn this. Come here." At long last, Rowan broke the stillness stalemate by waving for Brobson to approach.

This Rowan Monteagle was, save that one outburst, wholly unlike the Rowan Monteagle who periodically stalked the campground. *That* Rowan, the one with whom Brobson was familiar, seemed to find pleasure only at the decibel limits of the human voice. *This* Rowan, who had a temper as opposed to *being* a temper, was somehow even more terrifying. At least Brobson always knew where he stood with the old one.

Unfortunately, where the new one wanted him to stand was right in front of his desk. On trembling legs, Brobson stepped across the room, onto the bear's back. There were two large brown leather chairs on either side of him now, but Rowan didn't invite him to sit and Brobson sure as sugar wasn't going to be taking any initiatives in this room.

All at once, he recalled a reason to be scared. Belts with names, belts with names. He looked around the room but saw none. He felt them, though.

And heard them. "LUTZ," one of them cracked. Brobson came back to reality to see that Rowan's face could still move, as long as the move was towards anger. "Could you martial your attention for just a moment longer? As I know most of my vocabulary and syntax will be beyond your reach, here is what I propose: I will utilize an illustrative example. I will give you a scenario, and you will respond to my questions. In this way, we shall come to an understanding. Does this sound agreeable?"

"Yes, Sir."

"Good. Now, imagine someone has constructed a house on a sinking foundation. For the first several years, the house is as constructed. But it is soon pitched into disequilibrium. The house remains functional, yet there is just something incorrect about it. Years pass and exacerbate this core failing, until the entire home rests on an incline." He lifted his hands and tilted them to demonstrate, because that was apparently easier than choosing simpler words. "Now everything is crooked – beloved pets slide towards the lower end of the home, valuable porcelain rolls from the shelves, open windows on the elevated end invite rainwater and bird droppings. It is a highly unpleasant, and non-functional, state of affairs. Is this image of the crooked home fixed in your mind?"

"Yes, Sir," Brobson reported truthfully.

"Excellent. Well then, what do you do about it?"

"…Sir?"

"If this were your home, what would you do?"

"Move."

Rowan shook his head. "That's not allowed."

"Oh."

"You must continue to live in the house. It's the

only house you've got."

Brobson, temporarily forgetting to be afraid, locked the image in his mind and tried to look at it from every angle. "Is there a right answer, Sir, or is this one of those things where you can answer whatever you want and there's no wrong answer? Sir."

"There are wrong answers."

Well, that was *kind of* helpful.

"AH!" BROBSON GASPED after a minute of contemplation. "I got it!"

Rowan, who perhaps needed to martial his own attention, nodded with increasing purpose. "Let's hear it."

"I would go back and make everything crooked in the opposite direction. That way it would all be just like it was the same as if the house were flat on the ground. Sir."

Rowan frowned. "That's not right."

Brobson deflated. "Isn't it?"

"No. Then you're left with a crooked home full of crooked things. Why would you want that?"

"It could be kind of cool. Everybody in my neighborhood has like the same exact house, basically. Mine would be different."

"That's not what you want. That's not what I asked."

Enjoying the freedom from fear that this riddle had given, Brobson very nearly reminded Rowan that all he'd asked was what *Brobson* would do, which was what Brobson had just told him. But, fortunately for him, he remembered his place just in time.

134

"What you do," Rowan declared, "is deconstruct the house, dig out the foundation to whatever depth should be necessary, lay concrete, and carefully reconstruct the edifice. In this manner your home will once again become functional, and will not draw undue attention to itself, as in your non-solution."

"Oh. That just seems like a lot more work, Sir?"

Fast as a whipcrack, Rowan leapt to his feet and jabbed a finger at Brobson. "There! This is the problem. Are you now understanding why I have related to you through parable?"

Brobson shook his head. Remembering himself anew, he used his words: "Ah, oh, um, no, Sir."

"You don't want to do the work, Lutz. You're the house, was that clear to you? God built you exactly to specification, and then the rot of feminism and liberal bias ate away at your very foundations. Our job here is to take you apart, give you a Masculine foundation, and put you back together. It is not easy work, for any of us. It may surprise you to know that I find all of these things as unpleasant as you. But it is work we do, for God wills it. But I do not wish to see you dead of AIDS! I suffer from compassion. Yet you do not understand this, and so you talk of decampment. There is wordplay in that, though I understand it may not be plain to you."

"I don't understand that word, Sir."

"Fleeing. You want to run away."

Brobson wanted nothing more than to crawl into the pit that had just opened in his stomach. He had floated the idea, sure, but then decided against…

…who told Rowan? Had someone overheard? Or could it have been…

…could one of his four friends have ratted him out?

Whole body shivering, Brobson forced his jaw to snap out the words "I don't…I…who told you? That I did, but I don't!"

Rowan waved the question away. "A boy told Hal, who notified me."

It was even worse than he'd thought: not only had one of his friends tattled on him – the only counselor he'd thought was halfway nice in this place had helped!

Which of his friends had tattled? Scott thought the idea was dumb, but Brobson got the sense that he'd rather feel smart about himself and argue it away than simply tell Hal. Quazi had seemed much more on board, but the more Scott said, the less excited he was. Could it have been him? Possibly. As for Fred, w-

"LUTZ."

"Ah – hello, sir!"

"I am aware, from an account of the conversation in question, that the foolishness of your enterprise was communicated to you. So as I am eager to curtail my interactions with children as much as possible, I will simply impress upon you the wisdom of your acquaintances. If you cannot recall their points, as to the isolation of this facility and the cruelty of the wildwood, I would encourage you to follow up with them."

God, what he wouldn't give to find out who tattled on him, to imagine his face on the bag down in Dr.

Morzo's, so...

NO. Brobson clenched his fists so tightly he thought he felt blood. Or maybe it was sweat – his face and armpits were certainly going all in on that. He couldn't allow himself to be taken apart and rebuilt differently. He had already let them take him apart enough to put that idea in his head, to put that feeling in his heart, the mad happy feeling...

"What did you say, boy?"

Brobson let out a single braying cry. Oops. He'd accidentally said 'no' out loud. "I wasn't gonna run off," he insisted through sniffs and snorts, "I was just thinking about it! Because Dr. Morzo makes me feel bad things and I don't wanna get taken apart, I just wanna be a crooked house with crooked things, I don't wanna be a man, I wanna go home and h-"

"AND BE EXECUTED BY YOUR GOVERN-MENT?!"

"MAYBE!" He wiped his nose with his wrist. "SIR!"

In that moment, Brobson discovered that silence can startle. Rowan didn't explode as Brobson had expected he would. He just stood, knuckles on his desk, staring at Brobson. He studied him for several more seconds, and then asked Brobson if he wanted ten with the strap or one with the buckle.

"What?"

Rowan opened the large bottom drawer of his desk, pawed at the contents for a moment, and removed a long, thick leather belt with a gilt silver buckle the size of an avocado. "This is Hezekiah. I have different belts with different names, but I know you know that. So I'm going to repeat myself exactly once more: you can take ten strikes with the strap…" he snapped out the tongue of the strap end, "…or you can take one with the buckle." He dropped the heavy buckle on the desk. Brobson could now make out the design – it was two snakes, each devouring the other's tail, circling the skull of a goat.

"No," Brobson repeated, this time intentionally.

He got three with the buckle.

HE EMERGED FROM Rowan's office looking like a bad taxidermy job. Hal approached him, saying something about how he and Brobson's not-so-friend were only concerned about him, they just wanted to ensure he never went out into the woods alone, they cared about him and feared for his safety, that was the only reason they'd tattled. Eventually Hal gave up and went in to Rowan's office.

Brobson heard all of that, but didn't listen. He didn't care to. All he wanted to do was be alone, forever. He could never be betrayed if he was alone.

Only, he couldn't be alone, could he? God would always be there. Just as God had been here, and permitted it all to happen. He had been given a piece of paper too, and He'd signed it just like Mom and Dad.

Everybody that Brobson was meant to love wanted to take him apart.

He walked out of the cabin, around the back, and off the path. Not thinking about it, feeling more certain

than he ever had in his life, he marched into the woods.
Alone.

TWENTY-FOUR

OR THE FIRST few minutes, Brobson was just taking a walk. He had a lot on his mind, and when people had lots on their minds, they took walks. So that was what he was doing. That was all he was doing.

He reached his right arm over his shoulder, investigating the meat between his shoulder blades that Rowan had so enthusiastically tenderized with his belt. His middle finger touched a soggy patch of shirt, and then journeyed just a bit further.

A fourth phantom strike snapped across Brobson's back. He fell to his knees, mouth agape, as though preparing to bob for rotten apples. He wanted to cry, he wanted to scream, he wanted to shout, for oh so many reasons. But he couldn't. All that came out was a choked gargling sound.

No, he wasn't just taking a walk. He was running away. And why shouldn't he? Did he have friends there? No! Did he have anyone he could trust? No! Did he have anybody who would probably even care if he was gone, or notice? NO! When Mom and Dad came to pick him up, they would find out that he'd left and they could just make a new son who wasn't such a sinful little waste of life.

Pushing himself back to his feet, brushing the dirt from his knees, he made himself say it out loud. "I'm running away." A smile threatened to sully his gloomy countenance. "I'm doing it! I'm running away!" The threat became a promise. Better than that: a *fact*.

There was a difference.

Ok...so...where was he going?

He took a deep breath, and let the world know. "I'm running away to my Aunt Matilda's house in Phoenixville." There. It was official. He couldn't chicken out now.

Naturally, this raised the question of how exactly he was going to get to Phoenixville. Or how he would find his Aunt Matilda's house once he got there.

Ok, ok, one thing at a time. The first thing was just getting out of First Stone. He'd walked for a few minutes, so he was probably like two miles away from the camp or something? 'Four minute mile', that was a thing that people said sometimes. If he hadn't been walking for eight minutes, then he'd come close.

See? Already things were coming together. The thing to do now, then, was walk around the whole camp,

142

back to that big long driveway. He had to make sure he went far enough around to get past the part with that booth where Ted, and the guys who probably had guns to shoot kids on sight, worked. Once he got around them, it was a simple matter of following that driveway back (he would walk sort of next to it but not *on* it, so he could hide if a car drove by) until he got to the highway. Then he could probably take a taxicab to Phoenixville.

Brobson considered saying all of this out loud, but opted against it. The forest had gotten the measure of his conviction. Offering his itinerary would rather diminish that. So he set his jaw, rose to his full height, and began his journey by walking in the direction of the driveway. Which, if his memory served him, was left.

GOD SURELY FAVORED the residents of Pennsylvania, because he gave each and every one of his children a forever map of their home. This was how that similarity between the left hand and the Keystone State had been pitched to Brobson. How disappointing it had been, then, to discover that God must not have loved Pennsylvanians *all* that much; when Brobson needed a state map the most, his left hand just looked like a hand to him.

Yet it hadn't when Old Fath...Real F...*DAD* had broken the analogy down for Brobson. "Up by the thumb is where Lake Erie is. We live *here*. Pittsburgh is over *here*. Philadelphia is down *there*. Oh hey, you've got a freckle right where Phoenixville would be! That's

143

where Aunt Matilda lives!'"

Was there something providential in the placement of this freckle? Brobson pondered this as he stumped through the soft undergrowth, staring at his left palm like a mime watching a mime movie on his mime phone. Had God planted it there so that Dad would point it out to him, so that Brobson would know that the only safe place for him in the whole world was on the bottom right of the state? It certainly seemed possible. Except it had also seemed like God was pretty heavily involved at First Stone, in at least a consultant capacity. So…what did *that* mean?

That was a question for another day. What mattered now was getting out of the forest before nighttime. What were Scott's rule of threes? Specifically the first one. Three hours without shelter, wasn't that it? You could live three hours without shelter at nighttime, and then you died. Since he didn't know the first thing about finding shelter in the woods, his options simplified: get to the driveway/highway/away in the next few hours, or else wait for the sun to go down, stumble through the forest in the dark for three hours, and then die, probably from a bear or something.

Brobson lowered his hand, wincing as he did. The worst part about the pain in his back (aside from the sting of his sweat dripping into the wound) was that he couldn't see the damage it celebrated. He'd poked at it enough to know that it was bleeding; pretty badly, from the feel of it. His shirt was sticking to his back, drying on, celebrating his every move with a nostalgic little stab. It wasn't that he *wanted* to see a big gnarly wound on his back. It was just that, well, by not being able to see it, all he could do was *imagine* a big gnarly wound that was almost certainly bigger and gnarlier than the actual thing. He hoped so, anyway.

Reaching over his head as before, he peeled the fabric away from his wound, wincing at the crusty little reports as much as the pain.

SOMETHING WAS WRONG here. He should have found the driveway by now, he was positive. Almost. He was almost positive.

He sat on a log and listened. One, two, three minutes passed. He didn't hear any cars. That didn't necessarily mean anything, right? Some fancy cars don't make any noise. He almost got hit by a Prius once; didn't hear it coming. For all he knew there was a whole Toyota motorcade whispering its way through the front gate to First Stone. He could picture it as clearly as the grisly canyon cleft into his back.

Of course, he knew better.

He turned and set off walking in the direction he was almost positive would *actually* lead to the driveway.

BROBSON KNEW HE was in trouble when, in trying to figure out how far he'd walked, he regretted not knowing his times tables.

Had he seen that log before? It looked familiar. But he didn't remember seeing that rock with the grass on it next to the log earlier. This was a different log, one with a grassy rock next to it. He tried to commit this to memory, adding it to the catalogue he had been assembling.

Alright, so the driveway wasn't going to happen. What time was it? He couldn't quite tell. The canopy scribbled out most of the sky, and what sunlight did manage to shine through was too tired from being tickled by the swaying branches to be of any help. Within the last few minutes a gust of cool nighttime had sliced through the mugginess, a visitor from the future with a dire warning and somewhere else it would rather be. Night was falling. When did the three-hour clock start? Brobson cursed himself for not asking Scott more follow-up questions.

Well, maybe he still could. It was a simple matter: go back to First Stone, hide right outside the little clearing with the cabins until everyone was asleep, then creep in and grab his sleeping bag. And then, while he was at it, ask Scott when...

But how did he know it wasn't Scott who'd tattled on him to Hal? He didn't think it was, but he couldn't be sure.

Alright, scratch that last part. Get the sleeping bag. It was a wonder he hadn't done that first thing. If he'd known he was going to be running away today, he certainly would have done more to prepare.

Turning around, he headed back towards the campgrounds.

THE FOREST WAS laughing at him. A full-throated, head towards the heavens, both rows of teeth on display *haw-haw-haw* sort of laugh. The trees, the birds, the ground beneath his feet, the whole world was roaring at his misfortune.

And why shouldn't it? If he didn't find the compound in the next five minutes, he might start cackling himself.

Time passed. The deadline elapsed. The humor of the situation continued to elude Brobson.

He was lost. He'd been wandering for *ages*, and hadn't seen the first sign of First Stone. Weren't these his own footprints he'd been following? Granted, they weren't very deep impressions, and there were a bunch of other plants on the ground…so maybe he'd just been following a darker patch of dirt. Or maybe he was following in some critter's footsteps. Or maybe he'd just been overconfident that what people did on TV was something people could do in real life, and he'd imagined the whole thing.

Maybe maybe maybe it didn't matter, because it all came out to the same thing.

He was lost.

And if Brobson wasn't very much mistaken, the shadows were getting longer.

TWENTY-FIVE

BROBSON ENCOURAGED HIMSELF not to panic, not because he *was* panicking, but because he knew that was what you were supposed to do. Never having considered himself a courageous person, he was astonished to find himself *not* running around like a yodeler fleeing an avalanche of his own creation. No, none of that: the only difference he registered between the Brobson of two minutes ago who'd been trekking back to camp, and the modern Brobson who was hopelessly lost in the forest, was that this new and screwed model had keener senses.

He watched a ladybug purposefully scaling a leaf. The greenery warped and wiggled under the weight of the ladybug, who persevered for what looked to be very good little ladybug reasons that Brobson would never understand.

149

He heard the rustling of something off in the distance, where the trunks converged to hide the rest of the world from Brobson, and he from it. Maybe a deer, or a raccoon, or a bear. This last possibility, too, he faced with a remarkable lack of distress.

He saw th...

Brobson blinked, stepping tentatively towards the object of his fascination. He crouched down, ignoring the flashing neon OUCH OUCH OUCH of his back. Why was he crouching? He didn't need to get close to the moss to see it hugging the trunk of the tree. It just ...he wanted to get a close look at it, maybe. Touch it. He'd never touched moss before. It seemed like something he ought to do, if he was going to be lost in the woods.

It was yielding and slick, a breathing sweater that needed another spin in the dryer. The perfection of its shamrock green revealed small orange and brown blemishes upon closer inspection. That was reassuring, for some reason.

What had Hal said? Moss always grows in a direction that indicates South.

...

Was it that moss grew *towards* the South, or *away* from it?

He pondered this with newfound detachment, marveling at how academic the question seemed. One way would take him towards Phoenixville – and so salvation – the other, away. And yet, he wasn't so much racking his memory as he was perusing it.

Why hurry? There was a beautiful clarity in his hopelessness. Brobson could probably scream for help and be found before too long – but then it wouldn't be just his back that'd be leaking like a freeze pop. He might be lost in the woods, but at least if he stayed lost, there was still a chance of his getting to Phoenixville, however remote. Sure, he might die. But if Rowan grabbed him by the earlobe and dragged him back to First Stone, he would very probably *wish* he were dead.

Nothing to lose and everything to gain.

Moss grew on the south side of the trees. Yeah! Once he stopped thinking about it, there it was. Funny how that worked.

Brobson followed the moss north.

BEING A KID from the suburbs, Brobson was no stranger to trekking through an untamed wilderness. There was that copse behind Mr. Nunes' house that seemed like it was blocking you from getting to the pool, but actually if you cut your way through it was a *shortcut* to the pool. If you wanted to get from Brobson's to Fischer's, you could walk up the hill and then duck between the hedges of that big house that belonged to somebody Brobson had never met, walk along Grandview for a while, then climb up *another* little hill and walk along the traintracks, which didn't technically count as wilderness but no trains ran on them anymore, so they were covered in plants and therefore were wilderness again. Granted you could also just follow the roads, or even simpler yet you could ask Mom to take you, as long as you never asked Fischer to be your valentine.

Anyway. Wilderness. Brobson had seen his share. But it had never felt nor looked nor sounded quite like this. The air was thicker, but in a way that made it easier to breathe. It was crisp and clear, even as it smothered him in more humidity than a hug from Aunt Lindy (*not* a cool Aunt). His every footstep was a delightful catalogue of everything beneath his feet, the snap of a twig, the whisper of the dirt, the rustling of the plants. There were a few treads that sounded a bit more like the doleful, splatting epitaph of a caterpillar, but by not inspecting the sole of his sneakers, he could write this off as the work of his overactive imagination.

What his imagination could never have supplied was the sheer amount of life (tough-luck bugs notwithstanding); plants with muscular leaves, trees tall enough to worry an airplane, plants more colorful than his friend Marcus' language, all acrawl with bumblebees and stinkbugs and ants and centipedes and butterflies and a quite a few others besides. He hated bugs, but that was mainly because they loved to fly into his ear and buzz him off. These bugs all had their own bug business, just like the ladybug. They didn't have time for him, which gave him the distance to appreciate their industry. Hard workers, all of them! Certainly harder workers than most humans.

He did see a daddy longlegs once, and went scrambling over a fallen log just to avoid the rock it had conquered.

After what seemed like hours but couldn't have been, as the sun still hadn't dipped low enough to turn the day orange, Brobson sat on a low, flat rock (cushioned with his trusty moss) to rest his feet and air out his armpits. Sweaty underarms, there was another new experience. Granted, he also had all the old favorites, sweaty brow and sweaty neck and sweaty crotch, so it was probably just a matter of time before his pits sold out and started doing the same thing as everybody else. Ever the glutton for punishment, Brobson bent his head down to take a sniff, but his back objected strenuously to the stretch the move required. So he relented.

It was a little bit concerning, how much he was sweating without having anything to drink. His throat wasn't quite *parched* yet, but it was certainly dry. Brobson had always measured how thirsty he was by how appealing a glass of water seemed at the moment. Milk was his go-to, 1%, none of that skim milk nonsense, but also none of that 2% insanity. 1% of milk was all a growing boy needed. When he kept his grades high and behaved well, his parents would occasionally let him have an orange soda, even though they often stressed the sinfulness of a carbonated beverage. Then you had your lemonade, your fruit juice, your all kinds of drinks. Faced with such a wonderful spread of choice, who in their right minds would ever willingly reach for a glass of boring old water?

Well, Brobson sometimes would, if he'd just come in from running around in the sun. Sometimes a glass of water just *hit the spot*, but *only* if the water was cold enough to fog up the glass. Room temperature water was *always* boring.

Brobson sighed. What he wouldn't give for a foggy glass of water right now. He looked down at his left hand, which bore almost no resemblance to his home state. If Phoenixville was down by the birthmark, and First Stone was…probably somewhere up here, on his palm, then he must be…down *here* by now, at the bottom of his third finger. He was almost halfway there! He c*aauuuurrrrrrrooooooooOOOOOOOOOO*…

A chill ran up Brobson's spine, kicked open the door to his mind and splattered Bosch-esque frescos of demons and monsters and torment all over the walls. By the time rational thought had wended up the skeletal staircase and fought to catch its breath in the hall, Brobson was already prepared to see the Four Horsemen themselves emerging from the thicket to shoot him with their pistols or throw coconuts at him or whatever they did other than show up.

The wake up alarm, his rational mind bellowed as it swung open the door.

Ah, of course! That was that howling alarm they sounded every morning to wake the kids up. Only…it wasn't the morning. It was much closer to the night than the morning. So why were they…?

Ah.

Right.

Brobson frowned at his misjudgment. He'd assumed nobody would care that he'd disappeared. He'd imagined the only danger he really had of being caught was if he went back himself, or called for help.

He really should have known better.

…OOOOOOOOOOOOoooooooooooooaaaaa…

He leapt off the rock and ran.

TWENTY-SIX

LIKE EVERYTHING ELSE in the world, the forest turned on Brobson. It slapped him with low-hanging branches, it tripped him with rocks and logs, it spun him around with its unending sameness. Now all he could feel was the rattling of his brain in his skull, the pounding of his sneakers on the yielding soil. All he could hear was his ragged wheezing, and the echo of Coach Duffy telling him to take his exercise more seriously.

And another set of voices, these much closer in time and space.

It was hard to place the voices, but they seemed to be coming from up ahead, on his right. Instinctively, he dove in the opposite direction. He came down harder and sooner than expected. His left ankle rolled, and so did the rest of him. He tumbled down a short hill, landed on his shoulder, rolled again, and landed on his face.

157

He slid the final few yards to the bottom of the hill, pushing himself up before he'd come to a stop. Feeling neglected, the gash in Brobson's back tapped him *hard*. *Don't forget me!*

To quiet his turned left ankle he favored the right, limping to the base of an especially massive tree. It was a thick, stumpy trunk with a gorgeous green afro, one that grew so expansively as to render the lowest branches reachable to Brobson. He grit his teeth and ascended, the branches warping and wiggling under his weight.

HE SCALED WELL up into the crown of the tree, which had to be at *least* two stories, and lay flat on a thick bow, throwing his arms and legs around it and holding as tight as his aching body would allow.

Laying like that, gulping in air as quietly as possible, he closed his eyes, opened his ears, and tried to get the forest back on his side.

Three minutes later, he was pleased to find he'd succeeded.

He heard footsteps coming from far below. Which direction, he couldn't work out, nor their distance from him. But they were unmistakably human, and just as unmistakably coming his way.

As if knowing they had been caught, the feet produced a voice.

"BROBSON!" it called. It was not a voice he recognized, probably belonging to one of the Staff Dads. Were they combing the woods for him, wearing

158

robes and wielding staffs, like evil mages in a fairy tale? It was an image equal parts chilling and amusing. Brobson hugged the tree like he feared it might pull away.

"BROBSON, WHERE ARE YOU?" Almost every part of Brobson was itching to call back; it was not in his nature to ignore a question tendered by authority.

"BROBSON, YOU NEED TO COME OUT RIGHT NOW." The voice sounded like it was getting farther away. That was the good news. The bad news was that Brobson felt something crawling along his left ankle.

"YOU'RE CAUSING TROUBLE," the voice continued, now sounding as if it was getting closer once again. "YOU HAVE TO COME BACK OR YOU'RE GOING TO CAUSE A LOT OF TROUBLE FOR EVERYONE."

He was causing trouble? The last thing he wanted was to make other people's lives difficult...

No! They'd made *his* life so difficult, so *miserable* that he had wound up in this tree, bruised and bleeding, with something crawling up his leg. All to get away from them! *They* had put him here, so here he would stay!

Brobson craned his neck around, slowly as he could, trying to mediate between his desire to see what was on his leg and his back's desire that he see nothing but the flaked bark of the branch.

There was a big, beautiful monarch butterfly on his leg, coming up to say hi. It flaunted its bright Halloween wings like a brand-spankin-new backpack as it trekked over the most painful region of Brobson's ankle, and onto the neutral ground of the back of his upper calf.

"BROBSON!"

Here he'd been worried about a centipede or a spider. Nope, just a butterfly. He smiled at it. It stopped, looked at him, and slowly bounced its wings down and back up. It was only then that Brobson noticed one of its wings was slightly bent at the top, creased like a dog-eared page in a treasured book.

It resumed its journey, scaling the low hill of Brobson's heiny and balancing half-sideways on his left flank.

"BROBSON! THIS IS YOUR LAST CHANCE. COME OUT NOW AND WE'LL FORGET THIS WHOLE THING HAPPENED."

Almost every part of Brobson itched to call back, yes. *Almost*. But there was a new little part of Brobson, one that knew how to scratch.

Or maybe it was an old little part, one he'd never known was there. Like a dinosaur skeleton that God had buried under your house to confuse you about how old the planet was.

It was odd, how God liked to hide things just to confuse people.

The bent-winged butterfly crawled onto Brobson's shoulder, looked him square in the eye. This did not look like a bug that wanted to sing him a song or help him learn to believe in himself. This was a bug that merely wanted to say *you're in my spot*.

160

Brobson frowned at the butterfly for a few seconds, as a receding voice threw Brobson's name into an apparently hostile wood.

After another few seconds of staring each other down, Brobson nodded at the monarch and shimmied down the branch. The butterfly fluttered off his shoulder, settled into its favorite spot, and watched the boy descend.

If even the *butterflies* were against him, then Brobson really was on his own out here.

He would not get to Phoenixville tonight. He could not return to camp to get supplies. He could not count on anyone or anything to come to his aid. Quite the opposite, in fact.

This was new; all his life, things had mostly been done for (or to) him.

Shelter, food, water. He'd never thought of these as needing to be *obtained* before. But he'd also never climbed a giant tree and been yelled at by a butterfly. These were just new adult experiences he'd have to make sense of.

Just in front of him, halfway down the final branch before an imposing five-foot drop to the Earth, was some kind of nut dangling from a surprisingly strong stem. Food! There was one of the three, already taken care of. He'd been wrong, then! The forest was all too happy to provide.

Brobson plucked the nut from the stem, licked it once, and spat. It tasted like nothing so much as the gunky, sappy stuff all over it. He rubbed the nut clean on his shirt and bit into it.

Something cracked. It wasn't the nut.

He spat again, this time with feeling, and hurled the nut into the forest. In so doing, he lost his balance. He slid down the branch, bark chewing up his legs, until he crashed back-first into the trunk of the tree. To keep from screaming, he bit his knuckles hard enough to leave marks.

Swinging one leg over, he repositioned himself sidesaddle and prepared to make that final leap to the ground.

Onto what? His rolled ankle? He couldn't well land on only his right, unless he wanted to bust that one too.

Whimpering slightly, he tried to cling to the trunk of the tree and use it to slide himself down to the ground. With no purchase for his hands or feet, he had to squeeze with his whole upper body. A flare of pain lit his back up. He ignored it.

As he lost his grip and scraped his way down the trunk, Brobson let himself be impressed that he'd managed to wriggle halfway down. The landing hurt, but less than it would have at the full five feet. True, his right thigh had been ripped up pretty bad – Brobson grimaced as, in the course of plucking out some thick splinters, he accidentally peeled off a quarter-sized flap of skin – but the blood was just sort of sitting there on his leg, not dribbling out or anything. He could still walk.

He'd successfully climbed up a tree, evaded pursuit, and climbed back down without really *really* hurting himself. He was allowed to be proud of that!

He leaned against the tree and looked up, searching the green for a splash of orange and black. Before long, he asked himself why. He didn't really care if that jerk-hole butterfly was still there or not.

TWENTY-SEVEN

HE RULE WAS that Brobson was supposed to look for shelter even before food or
water. But for another mile or so, the hier-
archy of necessity seemed to be exactly the other way
around. Encouraging though the shimmy up the tree
had been, it had been twice as exhausting. Brobson was
so thirsty that he decided not to drink his pee, opting
instead to spray it into a bush. That was how thirsty he
was. He had to *decide* not to drink his pee.

But as the sun dipped further down, now low
enough to peek at him from between tree trunks (and
sometimes doink him in the eyes with a well-placed bolt
of light), the forest made a convincing argument for
putting shelter first.

After the sun said sayonara and went to check on
other kids in happier states, the woods seemed to ex-

hale, as though they had passed the day sucking in their collective gut. The world turned a beautiful purple color, a soothing hue most commonly seen by fish just prior to biting on a massive hook. Bugs conspired loudly beneath Brobson's feet – perhaps plotting revenge for their crushed caterpillar comrades – knowing full well Brobson couldn't understand the language of his own humbling. Above his head, owls hooted and bats flapped. Brobson hadn't even realized there *were* bats out here, but one helpfully swooped down into his field of vision, for no reason other than to say *hello* to the new neighbor. Most distressingly, as the violet eventide ebbed into a deeper dark, things stirred just outside Brobson's vanishing field of vision. Most didn't sound too big, raccoons and beavers, the kinds of things with kickable heads. But some sounded bigger. And while not exceedingly well versed on what the woods had to offer, Brobson knew that there were coyotes here, and wolves, and bears, and Shivers...

Three hours to find shelter suddenly didn't sound so silly. It sounded like the worst-case scenario.

Frustrated at having been demoted to the least pressing of the three concerns, Brobson's tummy revolted, grumbling as loud as it could in hopes of attracting someone from First Stone. With placatory palms pressed against his midsection, Brobson quickened his pace as much as his ankle would allow, not having a clue where he was going, knowing he had better get there before what little light remained grew tired of him.

166

FOR A BOY as sheltered as Brobson, the term "shelter" implied some very specific things which the boscage was loathe to supply. Obviously he wasn't expecting to come upon an abandoned cabin, with a cupboard full of chocolate-covered pretzels and a king-sized bunk bed. But was a cave too much to ask? A nice big cave, without any mean old bears in it? Weren't those supposed to be all over the place in the woods?

Apparently Pennsylvania never got the memo. Where there weren't trees, there were rocks. Some of these rocks were titanic, larger than Brobson's own home. Which probably made them part of the ground, actually, as opposed to the rocks scattered *on* the ground. Probably maybe who cared, they were all the same when it came to shelter. Useless.

He considered climbing a tree. And why not? It had worked well before. Except back then, there hadn't been a million little monsters swirling around up there. Granted, there were a million and one monsters of all sizes down *here*, but if he were corned on the ground, he at least had more options for escape than *down*.

Vision was failing him, so Brobson made a decision. The decision was to find shelter right here, in this random patch of the woods. Because as far as he could tell, this was a patch no better or worse than any of the others he'd trekked through. He made a quick survey of his environment, snatched up a few big, flat leaves like the ones people used to wave at Jesus and his donkey, and settled into a butt-sized groove in a mighty tree's roots.

With a bit of shimmying, made infinitely more miserable by his ever-aching back, Brobson draped the fronds over himself and was shocked to find the arrangement agreeable. Yes, it was cold, but not *freezing*. Yes, the roots were hard, but so is a rocking chair. Yes, the woods were scary, and that's the end of that sentence. The woods *were* scary, and it wasn't until Brobson ticked the great big Shelter box that he could spare the attention to recognize just how very scary they were. A Shiver traced its skeletal finger down his spine...no, no, focus on something else.

Like how he had done it. He was on the path to freedom, spending his first night away from *them*. Which meant he wasn't on the path. He was there. He was free. *This* was freedom.

In the dark, branches rattled and twigs snapped. Because he was coming. Finchley was c-

Brobson shook his head and hugged the fronds closer to himself. No he wasn't. He wasn't real, so he *couldn't* come.

This was freedom. Wasn't it? Was this what he'd wanted? Or imagined? It didn't matter. This was the hard part, but on the other side there were no aching, belt-shredded backs, nobody telling you that they loved you as they drove away and left you to be hurt, nobody calling you a mistake and demanding that you fix yourself. This was worth it.

A cycloptic demon appeared right in front of Brobson, its fiery eye gazing upon his innermost thoughts.

Brobson screamed and slapped the demon's face.

While he was pleased at his reaction time, he was less

excited to discover that the slain hellspawn was, in fact, a friendly lightning bug.

It provided its own little funeral service, resplendent rear pulsing into slow, ceremonious extinction. Brobson found the display inexplicably touching. What a rotten kid he was, to cold-cock the little guy! Poor thing probably saw Brobson, scared out of his wits, and came over to relieve the Pre-Adamite black. And for his buggy trouble, Brobson cleaned the critter's clock.

But unlike the butterfly in the tree, this lightning bug had not a single word of contempt for Brobson.

The peanut gallery certainly had a lot to say, though.

An ethereal low-watt glow suffused the night in vanishing blooms, revealing a world in silhouette. *Here* was a splash of green evaporating off a big black blob – a shrubbery of some stripe. *There* was a knot of earthy bark against a shaft of shadow – another tree, and the wondering face of a squirrel. The fireflies didn't quite dance, but they gave Brobson a show nonetheless, like renegade Christmas lights.

Maybe this was their way of mourning their buddy. Brobson had anticipated retribution, a little firefly fusillade. Yet here they were, singing their silent song as one of their chorus lay broken and leaking.

Dazzled as Brobson was by this morbid celebration, a skeletal finger tapped him on the shoulder, reminding him that the fireflies wouldn't be here forever. Darkness would reclaim him, and so again would the things that thrived in it without defying it.

Curling up as tightly as he could, swaddling himself

with palms in his cradle of roots, Brobson's stupid idiot brain made a terrible association.

This was what Finchley Shivers was doing when he'd died. Actually, worse than that – when he was made to live *forever*. The guy had crawled under a tree, which Brobson hadn't quite done but was just one step away from doing. And then the tree had eaten him, and digested him and then all of a sudden Finchley *is* the tree, stuck that way forever, still alive, maybe screaming, living and screaming, knowing that nobody will ever hear him, nobody will ever know.

What if the tree against which his unhappy back was scratching was that very same tree? What if Finchley was in the tree, watching him? What if he wanted someone to come and join him, to keep him company forever and ever?

Turning slowly, so slowly that he could hear and feel every creak and crack of his neck, Brobson looked up into the tortured face of the tree. There wasn't really a face there – or rather, there wasn't anymore. But he'd seen it, out of the corner of his eye.

He lowered himself back into his seated position. Of course this wasn't *the* tree. What would the odds be? Like one in a gazillion. But one of those trees out there, shadows darting wildly to hide from little lights, one of those trees was *the* tree. The one with Finchley trapped inside. Living, screaming, waiting. Waiting for what?

For someone else. For Brobson.

What was that?

In one of those gentle bursts of yellow, Brobson

spotted something. There were three trees and several more yards between him and that something, but the *thing*ness of it was unmistakable.

He fixed his eyes on the spot where it had been, squinting at the looming of a deeper darkness, like the clenched fist of a giant. He waited for another firefly to illuminate just the right spot, to prove him wrong. To prove to him that he hadn't seen anything at all.

A lonely gust of wind spooked the trees on its way to find whatever it was looking for. Bugs chirped, birds chortled, something fuzzy sneezed. And yet the world for Brobson had fallen silent. There was only that hole in the night there.

A hole that *moved*.

It couldn't be a boulder, not one that shifted like that. This wasn't a settling rock. It was a *shrug*, absent-minded and easy.

Tears welled in Brobson's eyes, only indirectly from fear. He had gone nearly a minute without blinking. If he did, he knew, he might miss the moment of revelation, if one ever came again.

He dug his hands into his thighs, willing himself to keep looking, *keep looking*.

A million little let-there-be-lights rose, shone and faded away. None where he needed them.

Keep. Looking.

Through a hole in the trees, a creation. A bug lit up a face. It was a dry, peeling mien hewn into bark with a blunt instrument. Its features were uneven, its eyes set crookedly above a diagonal nose and an ugly scar of a mouth. The eyes cracked like knots in firewood, but they gave a cold, unhappy light.

And then it was gone.

Brobson wanted to scream, in the same way that he wanted ice cream. It would have been wonderful, but it was outside the realm of possibility at present.

That giant's fist, draped once again in shadow, rolled and shuddered. It rose up a few inches, then turned with impossible languor until its jagged tail faced Brobson. Finchley slumped and slugged his way through the woods, his passage marked by a terrible, longnailed rustling sound. The fireflies gave Brobson a few more fleeting glimpses. Finchley, whatever he was, looked like an oversized, overfed worm made of tree bark.

So he and the tree had come to some sort of understanding, then.

This filled Brobson with frigid terror, at the center of which was a little, ooey-gooey dollop of something inexplicably warm. It was enough to help his exhaustion lead the way to slumber, though his sleep was fitful and his dreams too close to waking life.

TWENTY-EIGHT

H E AWOKE FEELING as though he hadn't a-
slept at all. Stiff and exhausted, Brobson peeled the fronds from his sweat-sodden shirt and
struggled to his feet. Of all his body's manifold griev-
ances, the one that registered most forcefully was his
back. It *screamed* so Brobson wouldn't have to. The pain
seemed to have spread as well, with a blast radius stretching down below his shoulder blades, and onto the
right side of his torso. Slowly as he dared, he lifted his
shirt to sneak a peek at his flank.

A ropy red vine hid beneath his skin, ragged and
furious. He could only imagine what the wound itself
looked like now – and, unfortunately, he did imagine. It
was hard not to.

Grimacing and limping (though, wonder of wonders,
his offended ankle seemed to hurt slightly less today),
he weaved between three dreadful trees and searched

173

the ground. He wasn't quite sure what he was looking for, but he'd know it when he saw it. A giant bark-armored slug ghoul would undoubtedly leave a distinctive trail.

The floor of the forest, cast in icy hues, was littered with sticks, leaves, acorns, animal droppings, and an array of unidentifiable little plant doodads. What there wasn't was a clear, Finchley-sized slash through the woods. This was, in a bizarre way, disappointing. Brobson should have been relieved, he knew, that Finchley wasn't out here watching him sleep. And he definitely was.

Relieved, that was. *Brobson* was.

From right behind him, something growled.

Brobson spun around, slipped, stumbled, caught himself, and scanned the woods. Nothing to see, though that didn't stop the creature from grumbling once again.

His stomach. Aha.

With the sun out and more immediate things to worry about, Finchley was once again consigned to the playpen of childish fancies. Of course there was no colossal slug prowling the darkened wood. What a stupid thing to even consider.

This newfound confidence in the way the universe worked made it so much easier to ignore the fact that his earlier stumble was caused by a deep, wide depression plowed into the dirt.

FOOD AND WATER. Well, water and food. He needed those things, in that order. Three days without water, wasn't that it? That didn't sound all that doable – it felt like his throat was cracking and peeling even more than Finchley's face. Where to find water?

Well, moss on trees needed water, right? It would probably want to grow in the direction of water. He was already following the moss, which was convenient. Water and Phoenixville, here he came.

Distance and time didn't really lose their meaning, because they hadn't had much to begin with. The sun went higher, ducked behind some angry looking clouds, and came back out again. Wind blew and halted. Hills rolled up and sloped down. Trees dipped low and stretched high. Bees swarmed. Squirrels tittered. Through it all, Brobson plodded, his back zapping him with every indelicate footfall, his eyelids drooping from the tedium of nature's plenty.

At some point in time and space, Brobson emerged into a small clearing, the ovular, level sanctuary that featured in every single cartoon about woodland critters. A single fallen tree lay at an angle through the far tip of the glade, an earthy imitation of the shaft of light stamping a puddle of gold at the foot of a grazing deer.

Brobson blinked and shook his head twice. There were five deer in the clearing, ranged in a loose crescent formation, nibbling at the ground.

Any second now, a handdrawn bluebird with a song in its heart was going to strafe him.

With no small amount of frustration, Brobson was

forced to temporarily waylay his agony and acknowl-
edge that this was all terribly beautiful. Having done
this, he allowed himself to be *very* frustrated about the
fact that the deer could eat whatever they darn well
pleased off the ground, and here he was, una...

...

Brobson took a mental stock of everything he had
on his person (which was to say, nothing), and quickly
glanced around his immediate area, careful to make no
sudden movements. Nothing he could use.

He looked back up at the deer and frowned. The
Manly thing to do right now was clear. He should kill a
deer and eat it.

How? How could he do that? If he could catch one,
maybe he could strangle it? They had big necks, but if
he gave it an Aunt Lindy hug all the way around, he
figured he could close the windpipe. So he'd have to
mount the deer like a horse, or else they could just
punch him off with their little tapdancer's hooves. But
deer were fast – would he be able to get close enough?
There were two smaller deer, one medium sized, and
two big ones. Probably the kids, a teenager and the parents, respectively. A little deer family. Which would be
easiest to catch? Probably one of the kids. But how
could he kill a child in front of its parents? Maybe, by
running out, if he caught one it would scare off the
others. Then he could do it without them seeing. But
they'd still *know*, wouldn't they? When their son or
daughter never caught up, any hope that the chimp
child from the woods had popped out for just a cuddle

would evaporate. How could he do it? Not logistically this time, but like, ethically? How did other people do it, those Manly Mr. Survival Men who dressed up like traffic cones and shot deer for fun? Weren't they killing kids in front of parents, parents in front of kids, friends in front of friends, brothers in front of sisters? How did they live with themselves? How?

Brobson sighed, one eye twitching as the air clawed at his throat. If you had to kill a baby deer in front of its family to be a Manly Man, maybe Brobson wasn't cut out to be one. What was so good about being a manly man, then? Everybody always told him to be one. But he had no interest in shooting a deer in the head, or beating a punching bag with a baseball bat. So where did that leave him? How could he expect to survive, if he didn't kill the deer, if he didn't swing the bat?

The Bambi family, in response to some silent starter pistol, hopped off into the woods. He marveled at their agility, despairing at his own lack of the same…and then he saw sense.

Don't kill the deer. Follow them, because eventually, they'll have to drink water.

It was a doe brainer.

TWENTY-NINE

THERE WERE STRETCHES when it seemed the family of deer were taking their time, so as not to lose Brobson; there were others when they hopped behind a tree and *vanished*, leaving Brobson to wonder if perhaps they weren't playing a little deer trick on him. In each of the latter cases, though, he stuck to the gentle suggestions of their hoofprints, and invariably he would catch up with them again. But it was never easy. They were so darn sprightly, and he was so darn...not that. With each step, his back got a teensy bit hotter, and felt a teensy bit bigger. His pace slackened under the load.

But there they were, nibbling away at greenery. Did they like him, these deer? Did he annoy them? He puzzled over this for a few stop-and-starts. Eventually a possible, indeed probable, answer suggested itself when

179

he slipped on a slick rock, forcing his bum ankle to catch his weight.

"Oh, Heavens To Betsy!" he screamed, as Mom had instructed him. Finding this insufficient, he looked to his left, looked to his right, and then shouted "fuck" the way most people shout "hello" into the cellar of a haunted house.

Not only did a tree not fall on his head, not only was he not cooked by a bolt of lightning, not only did an infinite number of awful things fail to happen…but the deer didn't even turn to look at him. They must have heard. He'd said it fairly loudly, hadn't he?

"Fuck!" he repeated for the hard of hearing.

One of the does bent its ballerina neck around, gave Brobson a blank look, and returned to its meal.

Brobson laughed once, a loud, ugly clown horn of a laugh. Never in his wildest dreams did he imagine he would ever, ever have the courage to say that word. That went double for first uttering it while deep in the wilderness, following deer on the off chance they might lead him to a stream. He giggled and wiped the sweat from his forehead. "Fuck," he gleefully observed.

Two things occurred to him as a result of this. Thing the first: the deer were not aid sent from God. If they were, they would have refused him service after he said a swear not once, not twice, but *three times*. God liked to keep it PG (on the language, anyway), and after a bad experience with the apostle Peter, He had a strict three-strikes policy. Brobson had violated both, and yet there went the deer, frolicking away at a lazy clip just as they

180

had before.

It was remarkable to Brobson, given his upbringing, that he hadn't even considered the possibility of their divine provenance until he was dimissing it.

From this followed the second thing that occurred: the deer didn't like *or* dislike him. They didn't care about him at all. They treated him the way they did everything else in the forest. Sometimes he did something to startle them, or fascinate them, but after a moment or two they would resume their course. To Brobson himself, he seemed the most interesting thing in the forest. Not because he was himself – that would have been vain, which was another thing that bumped you right to the top of God's Naughty list – but because he was human. And humans, he had always been told, had been granted dominion over the fish of the sea and the fowl of the air, and also over cattle. It was weird that cattle got their own shout-out, but since that's which animal makes Hamburger Helper, Brobson couldn't blame the Big Man for deigning to mention them individually. Humans also got the creeping things that creepeth, which seemed a lot like getting socks for Christmas. Then again, Brobson had thought that before he saw the creepiest creeper who ever did creepeth last night, if indeed he had seen what – *who* he thought he saw...

Anyway. Point being, even if deer in the forest weren't specifically mentioned in that biblical bill of sale, the implication seemed pretty clear: humans ran the planet.

Someone had forgotten to tell these deer, apparently.

They could hardly have cared less about Brobson. And while merely saying the word 'fuck' had exacted a small physical toll on Brobson, the deer regarded it with the same amount of incredulity and outrage as they did a passing bird (brown, not blue) that sang with the confidence of one who doesn't realize their auto-tune got switched off.

Brobson wasn't as nearly as big a deal as he'd thought. Which, in some ways, was comforting. In others, it was terrifying – it was so much easier to imagine something terrible happening to a not-big-deal than to a regular-big-deal.

The warm blanket of collapse coaxed him towards a premature bedtime. *Just lay down for a moment*, the sirens sang. Just for a minute. No big deal.

Much as he loved the song, he couldn't figure out the melody. So he kept walking.

THIRTY

ROBSON IMAGINED HE would hear the river before he saw it, and so imagined that he heard a great many rivers in his pursuit of the deer. All turned out to have been trees, wind or imagination.

So what a great surprise it was, in more ways than one, when Brobson scaled a fallen log and dropped straight into a mute rush of river. He hit the water some seven feet below the bank with a graceless *splop* noise. The river, not one to turn the other cheek, slapped Brobson hard, popping the air out of his lungs, sticking him with a million little needles, blasting water into his mouth just to really let him know who was boss.

Brobson wrestled with the current, snatching shallow breaths whenever he had the rapids on the ropes. In a fleeting moment of supremacy, he stole a backward

183

glance. No sign of the deer family. The rapids dunked him again.

It was impossible to tell just how quickly he was being whisked downstream – the usual markers, like visual reference points and oxygen, were in short supply. There were a few helpful hints though, like the very sharp rocks he kept slamming into (surely one would need to travel a great distance to encounter so many very sharp rocks!), or the occasional overhanging branch for him to grab on to, and then try to scramble up as it clicked, creaked and finally cracked in two, sending him gasping back into the torrent.

Brobson was not a great swimmer. He'd had a few lessons, but rarely ventured out to the deep end without supervision. The good news was that he didn't have any opportunity to swim here – all he could do was fight to keep his head above water. Which, come to think of it, was basically all swimming was.

He fought hard and well, and at long last, the flow conceded this. Like the world's worst waterslide, it delivered Brobson one final thrill: it sluiced him between two flanking boulders, blasted him through a many-fisted fog, dropped him from a height of two Dads, and somehow bonked him on the back of the head with a piece of wood. But after that, everything was…still.

Brobson floated in a fantasy of glass – the surface a perfect pane, unbroken save his disturbances; the depths, a committee of shards, were eager to welcome the interloper. He stared up at the sky, a few vanishing pockets of cobalt smothered by God's belly button lint, and tried to make sense of what just happened, and more importantly, how it was possible to be in as much pain as he was, and not die.

AT SOME POINT, with the sun still high enough in the sky to check in on him (when the clouds permitted) and ensure that he was getting sufficiently burned, the bed of the creek-nee-river came up to let Brobson know the ride was over.

He skidded a foot or so along the stony bottom, the current still strong enough to give him a final slap on the back. This was enough to shatter his vitreous daydream; he rolled forward with a shout, planting his feet and stretching to his full height. The creek rose just an inch or two above his ankles. It was astonishing to consider how something so ferocious could – and, really, *must* – become something so weak beautiful DRINK-ABLE.

Brobson dropped to his knees, wholly unimpressed by the sharp pain and thin runlets of blood drifting off in the current to go play in whatever rapids might be downstream. He punched his hands down into the water. He felt the smooth pebbles dancing in his hands, and the grit of the sand wriggling between his fingers. He lowered his head more reverently than he ever had in his entire life, and dunked himself.

The water was the purest he had ever tasted. It was full of dirt and fish poo and who knew what else. It had texture, gristly and harsh. It was perfect.

He drank selfish gulps. It was the least the river

owed him. The water ran cool between his cracked lips, over his tongue, down his throat, into his stomach. He could *feel* it fill his belly, like standing next to an air conditioner when it first turns on. But inside.

After a few more droughts, he felt something else happening in his stomach, less air conditioner and more Dad's "famous" pork stew.

He wretched exactly once, and then threw up a whole lot of water, a minimal amount of food and a little bit of bile. The river whisked it away like it couldn't wait to show the ocean.

Brobson fell to once again, this time drinking in more paced, measured sips. Periodically he would stop and splay his legs, splashing his butt down into the water, the better to sit and imagine that he wasn't there. Not in the sense of imagining himself elsewhere – simply imagining *this place* as it would be, were he elsewhere. Which was to say, this place as it had been in every single moment in time except for this one. That tree that's always falling over in the woods, so people can wonder if it made a sound – this was where that happened.

There was a profound idiocy in recognizing the beauty of this place, given the circumstances. He knew that. But he also recognized that this was probably a sight few people on the planet had ever taken in, if anybody. How likely was it that anybody had ever sat *here*, in the middle of this weak little creek, and just goggled? It wasn't impossible. But it also wasn't particularly likely.

It was nice, in its own tortured way, to be here. How else would he have ever thought to just *slow down* for a minute, and repose in the silky hum of water tickling the bank? Or drink in a breeze heavy with verdure's rich, round perfumes? Or hear the tale told by scratches and scuffs on ancient trunks? Or taste the blood in his mouth?

Aw, jeez.

He frowned and stuck two fingers in his mouth. They came back bloody – not drenched, just a bit pink, as though he'd flossed for the first time in a few days.

Frowning deeper still, he looked back up to the wonderland in front of him. Only the wonder had slipped away when he wasn't looking. Now it was just a lonely little stream trying to mind its own business and not attract any undue attention, like Mom and Dad driving through what they liked to call 'rough neighbor-hoods', which as far as Brobson could tell meant areas where houses didn't have two-car garages.

Brobson slapped his own face, instantly regretting it; the sun had beaten him to it. This was hardly fair – the trees should really have been protecting him from burns, right? – but there was no sense whining about it. It had happened, like everything else. He just had to get through it. He had to.

Another gentle gust cut straight through Brobson's shirt, skin, and muscle, burrowing straight down to the bones, which they shook like a wrongfully convicted man at the bars of his prison cell. Perhaps the wind smelled lovely like the one a few minutes ago had, but what Brobson mainly got out of it now was a full-body tremor.

He was absolutely soaked, and while that wasn't necessarily catastrophic right now, it very well could be in a matter of hours. Now it wasn't just about shelter for the night – it was about finding a way to get warm. Or at least dry. If not, it might take him less than three hours to freeze, even with shelter.

As he limped and clambered his way out of the creek, he imagined himself nestled between two roots, his eyes wide open, his body still and lifeless. Just as clearly, he saw Finchley Shivers approaching again, cloaked in fireflies. Slowly, slowly, Shivers made his way towards Brobson's corpse. He reached out a long, ugly branch of a finger, and poked Brobson once. So cold was the body that the head snapped clean off, falling to the ground and shattering into exactly one billion pieces. Finchley Shivers shrieked in fright and slugged his way back into the woods. The End.

Brobson chuckled and coughed for a few precious seconds. It was funny to imagine Finchley Shivers scared. It was easy, too. The sun was still out.

Ok, so, he needed to get dry. He also needed to keep working his way towards Phoenixville. He *also* needed a way to carry water with him, so he could focus on food and shelter. But he *also* also needed a way to carry the water without exerting himself too much, and also without putting it on his back, and also without making his ankle worse…

He stared at the stream silently for several seconds,

puzzling over a solution to these problems. He stared and puzzled, puzzled and stared. After a bit more staring and even more puzzling, the solution came to him. Duh! He slapped himself on the forehead, said "ouch", and then instinctively scanned his surroundings for witnesses to his embarrassment.

Follow the stream. He'd followed moss and deer and gotten this far – why not keep it going? That way, he could always be near a source of water, and not have to carry anything. Granted, that would mean he was no longer in charge of where he was going – but had he ever been? The river had to go somewhere, and along the way to somewhere he was bound to encounter someone. It only stood to reason.

The fantasy of crawling over a final log and finding himself right in Aunt Matilda's backyard died a quick death. Right now, the priority was getting out of the woods, where- and however he could, as quickly as possible. Otherwise he'd be following his fantasy, in all the wrong ways. Once he was out of the woods, he could find a phone and call Aunt Matilda. Then it would all be over. It would all work out. As long as he could *get* out.

THIRTY-ONE

THE ROCK WASN'T a rock. If it *were* a rock, it wouldn't have attracted Brobson's attention. He had more than enough to worry about, limping naked along the crumbling bank of the river whose current he was now following, flapping his clothes around in the hopes that they would a.) dry or b.) turn into a hang-glider. His hands were, quite literally, full. So a rock like all the other rocks would hardly have earned a first look, much less a second.

But a rock that was not like all the other rocks on account of not being a rock at all – that was worth looking in to.

It was just a few feet to Brobson's right, which put him right between the not-rock and the definitely-river. It was a mark of his weariness that he considered not even straying far enough from his current path to investigate the anomaly, but curiosity prevailed. He

191

shouldered his way through a prickly bush and knelt down, picking the object up with two trembling fingers and one sturdy thumb.

It was an arrowhead. About as long as Brobson's palm, smooth and marble-hued, with gorgeous blue imperfections, just like the threatening sky. It was cool to the touch, almost as cool as it was *to* touch. This thing had to be, what, a bazillion years old? Brobson had heard of kids finding them, and assumed they were lying or confused. Yet here he sat, holding a piece of history he'd just happened to find sitting where it had been for a bazillion years when some poor Native American guy probably dropped it and spent all day retracing his steps to find it again. That guy never found it, nor did anyone else in history until little Brobson Lutz came galumphing through. Funny how these things worked out some times, wasn't it?

Apparently not, because Brobson didn't laugh. He just stuffed the arrowhead into his pants pocket (which, he was none too pleased to see, were still sopping wet) and resumed walking and flailing, periodically stopping to check that the arrowhead was still there. It was bound to come in handy somehow – and besides, whoever dropped it would probably be delighted to hear that it was going to once again get back to work after the longest sabbatical of all time (well, second longest – people had been expecting Jesus back any minute now for quite a while…). He wondered if the original owner of this artifact was in any position to hear about this. They probably hadn't ever heard about Jesus, so

192

probably not. Hm.

The water in the river remained as refreshing as it had been a ways back, even though the physical costs of the trips down and, more demandingly, back up the ever-steepening bank were threatening to outweigh the benefits. The blessings Brobson had received from Rowan's belt grew more Old Testament by the hour. It felt like he'd been giving a piggyback ride to a pizza fresh out the oven, with the cheese still molten and mottled golden brown, wafting the most glorious scents of heavens to BETSY he was hungry, *starving* in fact, in a way that shamed him for ever having used that word to say *sure, I am hungry enough to eat maybe half of my dinner.*

Water was taken care of, and shelter was probably something he couldn't really plan (though he certainly wouldn't wait until evening forced his hand this time). But he needed food, and fast – he might be able to survive for three weeks without it, but he imagined it would be three weeks of little more than him on his pizza-back, crying for help. His limbs grew heavier with every step – a few times over the past few hours, he blinked out of a liminal fugue state, frantically checking that he hadn't waded in to quicksand, or a swamp, or a big syrup spill. Big pancakes and syrup. Waffles? No!

He scanned bushes and trees for things that looked like food, but couldn't even find berries to worry about being poisonous or not. He tried eating a few leaves, because if it was good enough for deer, it was actually not good enough for him. They were sandy and dry, which his body seemed ready to counter by vomiting up some of its precious water. He stifled the gag reflex and collected a handful of leaves, which he took down to the river and dunked into the water. This time, he got them down. Or, for all he knew, he had missed his mouth each time and now the leaves were floating downstream. They did absolutely nothing, and cost him precious energy just to make them 'edible'. So that was a no-go on the leaves.

Bugs didn't do much better by him. He found a centipede that he instinctively kicked as hard as he could (then immediately felt bad about); he then came upon a stinkbug, which he recognized from the stinkbug siege of his...of Mom and Dad's house. This was fortunate, because it meant he was aware of the noxious smell they emitted upon being crushed, which is a wonderful defense mechanism for your stinkbug friends and family, but not *super* impressive as far as self-defense goes. He passed these by, as well. Finally, he found some kind of grub party. If he'd found them in a dead animal, he'd call them maggots. But they were in a dead tree, which made them...something else. He hoped. He really didn't want to eat maggots. Thinking them 'grubs' and finding it workable, he grabbed a handful and tossed them back like M&Ms. He wasn't able to stifle the gag reflex this time.

Plants were out and bugs were out. Was it too much to ask for some berries, or an apple orchard, or an Applebee's? He grimaced and plodded onward. Food. He should have known this would be the hardest one. Then again, how could he have? Food had always been the *easiest* one at home. So much food! Open any drawer or cabinet or closet and you were likely to find it, piled up on itself, rotting away, hoping to be one of the lucky few pieces that got to fulfill its gustatory purpose, instead of ending up in the garbage.

Garbage. If he could find a garbage can, he would fall upon it as though it were his backpizza. If he could find his *parents'* garbage can, he knew he would have a feast fit for a king.

After another half hour or so of salivating over garbage, Brobson found something else remarkable.

Footprints.

Human footprints.

THIRTY-TWO

THE FOOTPRINTS CAME out of the woods, danced a raucous diagram into the soggy riverside, and returned whence they came. They were made by somewhere between two and six hundred people. How do the guys on TV shows always know? They had Manly skills, that was how. Brobson didn't have those.

What he did have was a postlapsarian modesty, rudely reimposed by the evidence of company. He struggled back into his clothes. They were dryer than they'd been, but that wasn't saying much.

Brobson shivered and stared at the tracks. There were only a few groups of people who would be this far out in the woods. Most obvious was, bad people from First Stone hunting him. Only that didn't seem likely, because how could they have beaten him here? He'd followed the moss downward, and then he fell in the river and got swept even further down (all rivers flowed

197

down, it only stood to reason), which put him WAY down. Maybe even out of Pennsylvania by now. So how *could* they have beaten him here? They couldn't have, that was how.

So who else? The second group was lumberjacks. Lumberjacks sing songs and sell paper towels, and swing axes sometimes. That was all Brobson knew of their kind. Were they nice or mean? Didn't matter. An outside shot at kindness was preferable to the certainty of a belt buckle, so that was a no-brainer.

Lastly was hunters. He hoped it wasn't hunters because then he'd probably get shot in the head, which would be pretty lame after everything he'd been through.

Brobson leaned down and studied the prints some more. Did they have a lumberjack-y look to them? They looked big, but so did all Manfeet. Granted, there was nothing particularly Manly about them, nor was there anything *not* Manly about them…

He sighed and rose to his boyfeet, wobbling as he did. What it came down to was this: he was exhausted, dizzy, famished, racked with pain and simultaneously too cold and too hot. If there was the slightest chance that the makers of these prints could help him, that was a chance he needed to take. Worst case scenario, he could tiptoe back to the river and resume his course. And just to avoid getting lost again, he could use his newly found arrowhead to periodically trace arrows into the dirt, showing him exactly how to find his way. It was a no-risk, all-reward type deal.

THE VOICES BEGAN as indistinguishable from the din of the forest. Ever so slowly, the murmurs coalesced into human speech, still indecipherable but at least identifiable. This led to a maddening crawl towards clarity. Then, all at once, Brobson could hear everything.

The speaker was just on the other side of a low-hanging bough. Adrenaline spiked through Brobson, only to come back disappointed that *this* was all it had to work with.

Despite the leafy fullness of the bough, and the entirety of the cover it provided, there was something horrifying about being protected by something not connected to the ground.

Of course, Brobson's horror could also have something to do with the speaker being, against all the laws of the universe, Rowan Monteagle.

How? How could that be? How was that possible? Brobson's wet and wild journey through the rapids alone would have put a substantial amount of distance between him and camp in a short period of time. It was inconceivable they could have gotten ahead of him, even if Rowan and co. had somehow been able to follow his trail the way Brobson had the river. But that wasn't the case – they'd had no idea which way Brobson went. They'd have to be searching the entire woods! So how in the *hell* could they be here right now?

The answer, unfortunately, was obvious: *here* wasn't where Brobson had thought it was. So then where was it?

Eager for clues, Brobson got himself as flat on the

199

ground as he could and listened.

"…stigma surrounding it, when in fact it is no different from any other hobby." That was Rowan.

There was a moment of silence, during which squishing and tapping could be heard.

"Yeah," said somebody with a half-full mouth, "but," they added with another loud chew and a cartoon-volume swallow, "you can't blow yourself up with, like, a model train."

Rowan paused another moment to answer. "Your power source could malfunction."

"Coin collecting, then."

More squishing and tapping, which Brobson took to be the cacophony of a meal. Once again, his stomach roared in hopes of getting him caught.

Rowan made a little *hmmpf* sound. "Is the concern self-immolation, or that I might be seeking to produce an illegal substance?"

A new voice jumped in: "Nobody's saying *you* specifically, just…people."

"*People* have been doing chemistry in their homes for generations. Where do you think the practice began, prior to taking its rightful place as a field of formal study distinct from alchemy? I am merely heir to a proud lineage of independent minds seeking to reveal the true glory of God's works, removed from the secular strictures of the *so-called* institutions of higher learning."

"Right, and where'd you buy your little set again? Amazon?" This voice was much older.

The first unidentified man, self-appointed advocate

for the devil, adopted a solemn, gravelly croak one might have expected more from his client. "Um. Guys."

Rowan was not to be distracted: "As a matter of fact, I did not. I purchased it from a reputable brick and mortar establishment which specializes in a-"

"In home chemistry sets," the older man interrupted. Brobson suspected this was one of the Staff Dads – it was hard to imagine anyone else not being terrified of Rowan. Then again, it was hard to muster up the right sense of awe while imagining him, belts safely tucked away for the night, going home and making a baking soda volcano.

"*No*, in chemicals too volatile f-"

"Rowan," croaked the devilman.

"What?"

"I think he's behind that tree."

A moment of silence.

Rowan ripped back the low-hanging bough, like a murderer behind a shower curtain. He was hardly three feet away.

Brobson's adrenaline was pleasantly surprised: this little hunk of junk could move pretty well after all.

THIRTY-THREE

"HERE HERE HERE HERE!"

They'd brought some kind of loudspeaker with them, though from the way it boxed Brobson's ears and rumbled his ribcage, it may well have been whatever Gabriel-horn they pumped the wake-up alarms through every morning.

"HERE HERE HERE HERE" was all Brobson could hear (hear hear hear) as he leapt up and sprinted away as fast as he could. *This should be painful*, he thought as he jumped and juked through the roughage. *I shouldn't have the energy to do this.* And yet, there was no denying that he was rocketing over rocks and logs, moving faster than he'd ever moved in his life. Made sense – he'd never *really* been scared before. Not like this.

The sheer (sheer sheer sheer) surprise of his

203

appearance gave him a head start. The First Stoners all probably counted on another day of searching at least – that Brobson would come right up to them, and all but offer his own opinion in the great home chemistry debate, likely never entered their minds. Because, he ruefully conceded, it was dumb. It was a dumb thing to do.

But it was too late (and/or too early) to beat himself up about it. It happened, and now he had to run. At his heels were raised voices and heavy footfalls and cracking belts and zapping electrodes and rattling chains and *whish*ing guillotines and death rays and nuclear bombs and recorder recitals. If he stopped running, if he fell, if he slowed down, or if they sped up, he was done for.

What an idiot he'd been to give up the river for this. He'd done this to himself.

And what an idiot all over again to be following the arrows he'd scratched into the dirt with the arrowhead! He'd been doing it mindlessly, like every other blessed thing he'd done since he'd wandered out here!

Risking a glance over his shoulder, he saw that he'd somehow maintained his lead. It was only about twenty feet, but that was enough. Maybe.

The more he thought about what he was doing, the harder it became. But there was nothing for it – he needed to know exactly when to make his move. It would also have been helpful to know what the move should be, other than *forwardasfastaspossible*. But last night shelter had more or less found him rather than the other way around, so it wasn't unreasonable to hope for a repeat performance today.

Before long (and thank goodness for that – he could feel his old stabbing pains filing themselves back into points) he saw his chance. Beneath a thick brontosaurus leg of a tree, the roots spun themselves into a tunnel, one that looked just large enough for Brobson but too big for an adult. If he could only slip in there, he would be consumed by the tree just like Finchley Shivers had been, destroyed and reborn as a mind that can only know pain, for ever and ever, and maybe this was even the same tree that had gotten Shivers, maybe Shivers was still *in there*, that was his den and he was calling out for Brobson to come slither inside and learn what it truly was to hurt, or maybe it was *him*, and he'd slugged his way back here and pretended to be a tree just to lure Brobson inside, where he would find not peace but the distended landscape of human suffering made to writhe in synchrony to the arrhythms of his heart-shaped burl.

So okay maybe the tree would be his backup plan. In the meantime, Brobson kept running in search of literally anything else.

As his pace slowed and his breath thinned, he made his peace with the fact that salvation wasn't just going to plop into his lap. Time was too short for hope. What he needed was a plan of action.

This was a problem. He'd never had one of those before.

Step one was surely to take stock. Items he had at his disposal: an arrowhead. And…his shoes. And he knew all the states and capitals. Almost.

Ok, step two was…

…

Crap.

No, *FUCK*.

And then it hit him: a low-hanging branch.

It clotheslined him onto his back, into a cocoon of scratchy leafage. There exploded a fantastic galaxy of anguish, which promptly took a number and got in line behind the solar system of torment that was his left ankle. The ankle got to jump a few more places up the queue as Brobson immediately sprang back onto his feet and resumed running.

Except somehow, this time, he wasn't just running away from Rowan and the other First Stoners. He'd had a Bright Idea.

He remembered a tiny ravine he'd had to navigate on his way towards the worst decision he'd ever made. It was a long seven-foot-deep scoop out of the dirt, like once upon a time there'd been a creek running here. Now it was dry, which suited him right down to the ground; he'd had more than enough wet adventures for one lifetime.

As if conjured, there up ahead (as in, about two yards out) was that very ravine. This was doubly good news; the fact that he'd only spotted it moments before coming upon it meant his pursuers would too.

In slow motion, like the superheroes in movies he wasn't supposed to be watching but *duh* of course he'd seen 'em, Fischer *loved* those movies, Brobson tucked and rolled just as he reached the lip of the gully. As he did, he extended an arm and snatched up a big rock,

206

about the size of the baseballs he was supposed be throwing in gym class but *duh* of course he didn't, they always made him be batboy. Reeling it in to his chest, he spun in mid-air and slid on his right flank (one of the few parts of his body that still needed something to complain about) down the steep decline towards the once-upon-a-time creekbed, head first. Halfway down, he saw what he wanted: another cocoon of scratchy leafage deep enough to swallow him up (but not for keeps, like a tree). He armycrawled towards the bed of leaves before he'd even reached the bottom of the ravine. Dissatisfied with his pace, he snapped his arms and legs under him and leapfrogged into the bed. He landed on his left side, as the right had taken a number and gotten in line, and besides he was right handed. As he was vanishing into the green, he wound up and hurled the rock over the far side of the gorge, as hard as he could. He didn't keep his head up to see where it went: he ducked his head beneath the foliage, flattened himself as much as he could, and waited.

As he fought to silence his gasping and panting, and as the lately hurled rock *clack*ed against a tree, Brobson could not deny a startling fact: that was the coolest thing he had ever done in his entire life. Not even being cocky. That was awesome.

The real test, of course, was whether or not the classic decoy fake-out had worked. Even if his head weren't being shaded by the kindest living things to be found on the floor of this forest, it was at such an angle as to make visually monitoring his success impossible. So he listened.

Scrambling sounds. Branches being shaken. Heavy panting. Had they even heard the rock? Surely that detail hadn't been for nothing – that was maybe the coolest part of Brobson's whole maneuver. That *was* the decoy, that they would hear the *clack* and shout 'there he goes!' and then go running off in exactly the wrong direction. It really had been a textbook decoy fake-out. Brobson was really proud of it. He hoped they had heard it.

Tumbling leaves and ploughed soil. They were sliding down the hill. One guy grunted. Brobson didn't recognize the voice. More shuffling, twigs snapping.

They were climbing up the other side of the hill.

Brobson wanted to scream and shout, jump and jive, twist and then shout for a second time. But he sat on it.

Instead, he treated himself to a fireworks show and float in the Memorial Day parade, all in his head. He had done it! He'd tr-

"Excuse me," said Rowan's voice, "but where do you all think you're going?" This was the voice of a man treating himself to not just a float in the parade, but a whole procession in his honor.

A new number was called, and Brobson's ankle stepped up to register a grievance. Then order broke down, and everybody had their say at once.

THIRTY-FOUR

ORE SCRAMBLING NOISES, all of them descending. A great deal of laughter – mostly relieved, some of it with teeth. It was hard for Brobson to hear all of this, over the sound of his own whimpering. And growling. He was making noises he'd never heard himself make before, or even imagined himself capable of making. Naturally he was distraught at what he imagined would be done to him back at First Stone. He was also profoundly frustrated that the coolest thing he'd ever done hadn't actually done what it was supposed to do. In which case, it wasn't all that cool, was it? On top of that, he was ashamed of his cowardice, of having fled from something so many other kids were strong enough to endure.

There was also, buried somewhere not so deep in this soup of emotion, relief. This was perhaps the most distressing feeling of all.

He lay on the ground, vibrating and making strange noises, shaking his entire pathetic excuse for a hiding place. When nothing happened and continued to do so, he lifted his head and craned it around for a look.

Rowan and four other Men, including Hal, were just standing and staring. Upon seeing Brobson's face, Hal and two other guys went white. One had no reaction. Rowan's mouth merely flattened even more, his lips receding into his mouth. If that look corresponded to any human emotion, Brobson had never heard of it.

Brobson stared at the mouth, slowly lifting his gaze to meet the eyes. He gasped. Rowan's eyes, which Brobson had only ever thought of as something from which to avert his own gaze, weren't fiery or stony or any of the other things that the surrounding face could often be. They were weary and wet.

In a single instant, Brobson recognized Rowan's dread secret, his Achilles heel. He inculcated fear and intimidation to discourage kids from looking at his eyes. There was so much humanity in them, so much compassion, so much anger. So much belief. So much. Easier, then, to be the boogeyman. Otherwise he might have to learn how to talk to children.

There wasn't anybody on this planet Brobson was prepared to feel more sorry for than himself just then. But he did spare some pity for Rowan. Why, he couldn't begin to imagine. But there it was.

Rowan sighed. "Do you know into what you've gotten yourself, Lutz?"

Brobson shook his head. "I'm not going back.

210

You're all really bad people and I'd rather d-"

"I'm sure you misunderstand me. I'm asking if you're familiar with the genus of vegetation in which you have attempted to conceal yourself."

If there was a point, Brobson couldn't see it. He could, however, feel those well-filed points of pain. The rush was over now. Boy, was it ever.

His left arm, propping him up in this awkward position, quivered. He could see it shaking the leaves, which were dumb leaves and who cared, what was the point?

Still making no moves towards Brobson, Rowan stretched out his arms, palms down. As he spoke, he flipped them up slowly. "*Toxicodendron.*" He lowered them back to his sides. "I'd assay the species as *radicans*. But do not quote me on that. Ha." The ballpoint mouth creased upwards: that was apparently some kind of joke. Brobson was heartened by the fact that nobody else smiled. "*Toxicodendron radicans* is likely familiar to you by its colloquial sobriquet, 'poison ivy'.

"I say all of this," Rowan continued, "to underline the fact that you are going to develop urushiol-induced contact dermatitis, a discomfiting irritation of the skin. This is inevitable, given the coverage and duration of your exposure. I'm certain that this pales in comparison to some of the other physical traumas you have quite evidently endured. But, and there is no noble way to articulate this, we have not endured these same traumas. Which would make a discomfiting skin irritation very discomfiting indeed. Relatively speaking, we would actually find it *more* discomfiting than you likely will.

So," he concluded as he somehow straightened his back even more, "we would all be exceedingly appreciative if you would remove yourself from the *Toxi*-er, poison ivy, so that we will not be compelled to effect your removal by force, and so expose ourselves to urushiol-induced contact dermatitis. A discomfiting irritation of the skin."

The two stared at each other for several seconds, Brobson lying on the ground, Rowan crouched down just beyond the reach of the ivy.

Brobson said "no".

Rowan considered this by trying to look at his own eyebrows. He closed his eyes for a moment, and reopened them with his sights once again set on Brobson. "If you do not remove yourself, I shall assign Hal the task of extracting you."

"I don't care."

This seemed to genuinely surprise Rowan. "I was under the impression that you favored Hal?"

"Not anymore."

"Hm."

From the far side of the gulch, where that stupid rock that Brobson had thrown, like an *idiot*, had made its useless *clack* sound: voices raised against a gathering wind.

"Down here!" cried one of the older men in Rowan's entourage.

The distant voice asked a question.

"HERE!"

Rowan's eyelids drooped. He looked at Brobson the

212

way people in workplace comedies look at the camera. "Climb up and provide a visual component to your summons," Rowan suggested over his shoulder.

"Good idea. Say, you're taller than I am, aren't you?"

Ah, so this was probably the old man who'd been razzing Rowan about his leisure activities. Brobson liked this guy.

Not taking the bait, Rowan turned to Hal and waved him over. Demonstrating the First Stone chain of command, Hal complied without a word out of turn.

As if all he'd required were an example, the older man swallowed his pride and climbed up the wall of the ravine, shouting "HERE" as he did.

"Hey Brobson," Hal mumbled.

Brobson just stared at him. His shoulder was killing him, but now wasn't the time to reveal any weakness. He could lie down was he was dead!

Hal sighed. "Come on, man."

Still, Brobson stood firm. Well, not stood. Nor was he firm. But he was still.

Hal gave Rowan an imploring glance, to which the head counselor replied with a remarkably apologetic slope of the brow. So it was a bluff that Rowan had not anticipated Brobson would call.

More scuffling and sliding announced the arrival of a second group of searchers, this one slightly larger, at seven people. They followed the older man back down into the ravine – all except one, who stood at the top of the hill, staring down.

"What's he doing down there?" This hesitant man

213

on the hill asked. He was dressed in an aggressively tailored suit, just as he had been the last time Brobson had seen him. Unlike last time, however, this suit was jet black – no way a white suit would get through the woods uncrudded. That was the Reverend Dr. Keith Malamar's sole concession to the great outdoors, however. He was still dressed to the nines, jacket, tie, and all. Brobson couldn't see his shoes from where he was, but he had a pretty good idea as to how appropriate for hiking they were.

Before Brobson could ask the Reverend Doctor what *he* was doing up *there*, or out here at *all*, Rowan turned and said "he's lying in *To...*in poison ivy, hoping to exhaust our patience."

"Well," Malamar helpfully suggested, "get him out."

"That is precisely our current endeavor," Rowan replied. He turned back to his current endeavor.

Malamar clapped his hands together. "Hey!"

Rowan tilted his ear towards Malamar, but refrained from subjecting his neck to any undue strain.

Brobson, able to exercise no such restraint, watched the Reverend Doctor shuffle angrily from atop his natural stage. "Don't pull your five dollar word routine with me. Words are my tools. You might be able to talk over everybody else's head, but you won't talk over mine!"

Another dry almost-smile. "How could I speak over your head," Rowan wondered, "when you're all the way up there? Ha." He said this in an indoor voice, and though Malamar bristled at the comment, he pretended

214

not to hear it. For now, at least. That had been another helpful demonstration, this time on the complexity of power delegation.

Rowan showed Brobson both sides of his smile. "You see what I am required to tolerate. I understand the quality of your resentment."

"Oh," Brobson sneered, "how big is *his* belt buckle?"

The smile vanished, which was gratifying. "Corporal punishment is extreme but efficacious. It is hardly surprising that, during our most formative years as a nation, the practice was accepted as an essential component of responsible child rearing. Do I take pleasure in it? Certainly not. B-"

"You have names for your belts."

A couple seconds of silence. Then, "…an organizational convenience. I know you find this difficult to accept, but I have your best interests at heart. I am in no way obligated to inform you of this, as I consider it a weakness. But I do sterilize the belts' buckles after each conversation. So you see. The manner in which I provide guidance is not thoughtless. I only want to make you well."

"I'm not sick!"

Rowan put his hand to his neck, as though checking his pulse. He stared over Brobson, down the path carved out of the woods by a long-vanished stream, searching for something. Eventually, he found it. He stood back up. The popping of his knees startled Brobson.

With a nod to Hal, Rowan turned and walked towards Malamar.

Hal crouched down by Brobson. "Dude. Please. Just get up."

"No."

With a guttural *uugghh* noise like Mom made when she was fed up with the computer, Hal leaned forward, plunged his arms into the ivy, and clamped his hands around Brobson's shoulders. He heaved them both up and out.

"Anybody got some barrier cream or something?" he wondered as he walked away from Brobson without a second glance. Hal was the only one feigning indiff- erence: everyone else, about a dozen people so far with still more raised voices calling out from the ass-end of the afternoon (drifting towards the evergreen beacon of "HERE!"), was fixated directly upon him. Never had such a large group expressed such interest in little Brob- son Lutz. He would have given anything in the world to melt into the ground, or turn into a frog and hop away, passing the rest of his days eating flies. Anything to not be here, in the basin of a gulch, with a gaggle of grown- ups making angry faces at him.

THIRTY-FIVE

THE REVEREND DOCTOR Malamar sulked, his arms folded, just as he had been as his posse struggled out of the ravine with Brobson in tow. "Is he dying?"

One of the guys who came in the third wave of searchers, a little gnome named Doering who was neither Young nor Old, was apparently the camp's nurse. He had asked to see each of Brobson's wounds, tutting and harrumphing as he inspected the boy like he was valuating an antique. Brobson resisted for as long as he could – Dr. Morzo's reign of terror went on quite literally under Doering's nose, which tainted him by association – but the nurse seemed genuine, and Brobson was tired.

"The wound on his back is definitely infected," Doering announced with a sidelong look at Rowan, "and he's got a nasty gash on his leg that could well go the same way. He's rolled his ankle, but th-"

"Sure, sure," Malamar cut in, "but is he *dying*?!"

Doering took a deep breath, exhaling it as "no."

Malamar threw his arms into the air. "Then what the hell am I doing here?!" This he exclaimed with his own look towards Rowan, less sidelong and more head-on.

"I apprised you of the situation," Rowan explained patiently, "and you determined that your presence was required. I can't speak to your reasoning."

Malamar shook his head. "Jesus, Rowan." Rowan flinched at the mention of one of these two names; Brobson couldn't be sure which. "My lawyer's squawking about this could be a liability issue, because we don't have fences on the camp. Why don't we have fences on the camp?"

"I believe it was due to a budgetary disagreement," Rowan replied icily.

Malamar brushed this away. He turned to Doering. "I'm assuming there's no way to make the kid good as new before his parents pick him up, is there?"

Doering's reply came in the form of boggling eyes.

Rowan shook his head. "Even if it were, it's inevitable that one of the other children will mention this to an unsympathetic acquaintance, at some point. It's too dramatic an occurrence to not wish to share with one's peers."

"What about the waiver?" Malamar wondered. "The parents sign a waiver, right?"

"For minor contusions, received in the course of

218

corrective therapy," Doering recited in a spiteful impression of Rowan. Resuming his own voice, he added, "this isn't covered."

"Alright, alright. Honest assessment, then: how connected are this camp and my name?"

Rowan made a face. "You didn't ask your lawyer?"

"I'm asking *you*."

"Too intimately to divorce yourself from it. If that is why you're asking."

"I'm just asking to ask."

Everyone stood in silence for a moment. Brobson, feeling emboldened by the remarkable amount of tension between these grownups, broke it. He stared at Malamar until the Reverend Doctor noticed and returned his gaze.

"You talk better when there's a camera on you," Brobson observed.

Doering, tending to Brobson's wounds with his back to Malamar, smiled at this. That was enough to keep Brobson strong as Malamar whisked down from his mountaintop and slapped Brobson hard on the cheek.

"HEY!" Doering cried, physically shoving Malamar back.

"Don't push me!" Malamar screamed.

"Don't slap my patient!"

"Oh, so it's alright for Rowan to beat the kid with a belt, but as soon as I put hands on him, you've got a problem?"

"Once he's my patient, nobody puts hands on him. Got it?"

"Consider yourself fired."

"That's your move, is it? Phase one of your PR blitz?"

Rowan, like a referee at a hockey game, watched and did nothing.

Malamar shook this off, and once again knelt down by Brobson. Doering raised a defensive hand, but the Reverend Doctor shoved it away. "I had to break contract on a very lucrative and important speaking engagement to be here," he snarled, "so you're welcome. Now you owe me one. Ready? You're gonna tell everybody that you got lost, *not* that you ran away with your limp little queer dick hanging between your legs. You fell a lot, got attacked by a possum, I don't give a shit. But every scratch on you happened out here in the woods. That's what happened."

Tired, hungry, pained, cold, Brobson didn't have the energy for another courageous act of defiance. He nodded his head, if only because that way gravity did half the work. He crossed his fingers, though. If anybody noticed, they didn't say so.

"Are you done?" Doering asked.

Malamar grunted, rose to his feet (which were indeed stuffed into idiotically dressy shoes) and walked away.

The nurse turned towards Rowan. "We need to get him back to camp. He needs antibiotics, just for a start. I can dress his wounds right now, and we can get him some food. That's about all we can do out here."

Rowan nodded his assent, folded his arms, and

unfolded them. "I don't think we'll have much difficulty persuading Keith."

Satisfied with that, Doering turned to Brobson, gently laid a hand on his shoulder, and asked him a question no adult had ever asked him before, at least without immediately answering for him in the negative.

"Are you okay?"

Brobson cried ugly.

THIRTY-SIX

THEY WERE ALL trekking back to camp, Hal leading the way, Malamar close enough by his side that he could look as though *he* were steering the ship.

And then, in an instant, they weren't anymore.

The shift came when Hal looked down at his compass, stopped walking, and said "huh".

The amorphous splatter of searchers jostled to a halt, Brobson in the middle, flanked by Doering and Rowan.

"What's 'huh'?" Malamar demanded.

Hal looked up, squinting between the trees.

Malamar turned around. "What's his name?" he shouted to Rowan.

"Hal," Rowan offered.

"Hal!"

Hal jumped. "Huh?"

"I asked you a question," Malamar growled.

223

"Oh, right. Um. We should have reached our first marker by now."

A murmur shook the nearest congregants behind him, and spread.

Their collective discomfort was manna to Brobson, even as he drank from the same unwell.

As the day backslid towards evening, it took the color of the wood with it. Those few patches of sky visible through the growth were suffused with ominous puffs of tarnished silver. The wind had picked up, now strong enough to tousle even Malamar's gel-crusted hair. It was going to rain soon. And they should have reached their first marker by now.

Malamar examined Hal like he was looking for the perforated TEAR HERE flap. "Well, we haven't. So what does that mean?"

"Um…"

"Are we lost?"

"…"

"JESUS CHRIST," Malamar called. When nobody answered, he stormed through the parting seas of the party, straight for Rowan.

"Your boy's gotten us lost," he snapped.

"I heard," Rowan replied. He didn't sound nearly as upset.

"So now what?"

"We pitch a few tents and wait out the inclement weather that looks liable to break at any moment."

Malamar physically recoiled from the suggestion. "I'm not sleeping in the goddamned woods! Over-

224

night?!"

"Everyone else already has. Especially him," Rowan added with a gesture towards Brobson.

For his part, Brobson couldn't help but feel a little bit bad for everybody here. They'd all had to sleep in the woods because of him. Then again, he'd had to sleep in the woods because of *them*, so that was a wash.

"Yes," Malamar recovered, "what *about* him?" He appealed to Doering. "We've got to get him to a doctor, yes? A *real* doctor?"

Doering smiled. "Quite right, as we've only a registered nurse and a TV preacher with an *honorary* doctorate out here, but if the weather breaks and Brobson's left exposed to the wind and the rain, he might be in worse shape than if we hunkered down. We can at least warm you up and get some food in you. What do you say?"

Five seconds after that, Brobson realized that at some point Doering had starting talking to *him*, and concluded by asking for *his* opinion. "Ah? Oh. Y…yes. I'd like that, please." Much as he didn't want to go back to camp – because camp meant home, and home very likely meant another camp, in one form or another – he *did* want to eat. He *did* want to be warm. He couldn't help it.

Doering looked to Rowan. "Well, there you have it," Rowan said. And then, like a werewolf, he transformed back into Rowan Monteagle, Head Counselor. "ATTENTION," he barked to the assembled, "we're bivouacking for the night! Fan out, observe protocol,

225

and locate a suitable clearing in which to situate our camp!"

Everyone scattered, presumably to 'observe protocol'. Rowan stormed after a larger clutch of them, shouting more words he got off the TV.

Malamar, stood between Brobson and Hal, whipped his head back and forth, unable to decide who most deserved to behold his contemptuous wrinkles. Hal made it easier by brushing past him, not having the decency to look even a little bit cowed, and stepping right up to Brobson.

He and Doering exchanged meaningful glances.

"That's the best I can do," Hal mumbled through pinched lips. Then he was off, to get yelled at by any number of people.

Brobson puzzled over this. What was the best? What had Hal done? He'd gotten them lost. So how was that the best? How was…?

…

About ten minutes after that, the first rumble of thunder shook the trees. Which was remarkable, because for Brobson, the lightning had struck long ago.

THIRTY-SEVEN

NOBODY ELSE COULD see him. They were busy moving sticks and rocks around, and yelling at tents. But even so – how could they not *see* him?

Brobson could see him. He couldn't do anything *but* see him. He stared, too terrified to look away and ask Doering if he could see him, too scared to even blink. He was afraid that Finchley would be right in front of him when he turned back. He was just as afraid that he wouldn't be there at all.

Finchley Shivers was a bit easier to make out in the royal dusk. He was still mostly silhouette, but at least now he was casting his own shadows.

He was at least seven feet tall, a human face chiseled into bark and set in a cowl of timber. His body, hunched and covered, was more armadillo than slug (but still, a fair amount of slug), but there was enough human

227

about it to be truly disturbing. Beneath his ligneous shell was a small, equally flammable body. Two stiff, squat legs, only about the size of Brobson's taken from the knees down, supported the majority of his bulk. His arms, hideously long and triple-jointed, reached from just beneath his head all the way to the ground.

Finchley had gotten trapped in a tree, alright. But through sheer force of will, he had imposed his old shape upon its ancient intransigence, and taken it for a walk. There was something to admire in that.

Brobson sat at the edge of the clearing one of the searchers had located, eyes trained on Finchley. There were still a number of trees between them, and this wasn't the best light…but what kind of expression did he have on his knotted, twisted face? Was it amusement? Pity? Pain? Concern?

It could have been any number of things, but one thing he was fairly certain it *wasn't* was fury, or anger, or hatred.

Why, exactly, had Brobson been frightened of Finchley? Had there been anything in the story that demanded terror? Or, had he just sort of… assumed?

A bizarre thought occurred to Brobson: had Finchley been looking out for him this whole time? Was that how he was still alive? Should he be rushing over to that poor creature and embracing him?

Brobson surprised himself by taking a few tentative steps towards the treeline (not going too far – that would freak everybody out, and he wanted them as un-freaked as possible) and calling out: "Are you real?"

Finchley Shivers smiled. Brobson could hear the groan of his splintered jaw warping in mirth.

"Answer me!"

Nothing.

"Don't you know how to talk?"

"Ku," Finchley replied, with astonishing effort. His voice was as smooth and clean as any Brobson had ever heard. It was, in fact, one of the most gorgeous things he had heard in his life. But to merely exercise it in the service of a nonsense syllable seemed to cause Finchley a literally unspeakable amount of pain, his already demented features rearranging themselves ever so slightly in the attempt. It was like witnessing an opera singer being fed feet-first into a woodchipper.

Knowing full well he would get no comprehensible responses, Brobson nevertheless continued his inquiry. "What d-"

"Brobson," Doering said with evident concern, "who are you talking to?"

Startled, Brobson jerked around to look at Doering. He cursed himself – he knew that when he turned back, Finchley would be gone. That was just how these things worked. And if he pointed to the woods and said 'I was talking to *him*,' Doering would think him delirious and potentially favor him with more intense observation. Which, though the man seemed sympathetic to him generally (why else the meaningful looks with Hal?), would probably squash any miniscule hopes Brobson had of getting away again tonight.

And maybe he *was* delirious. It certainly wasn't outside the realm of possibility that Finchley wasn't real. After all, assuming Finchley *was* real, he couldn't utter so much as a single noise without subjecting himself to excruciating pain. He was, practically speaking, unable to speak. So how could he tell anybody his story? Because, if the point was that he crawled into the tree when nobody was looking and got swallowed up, how could anybody know the story if he hadn't been able to tell anybody about it? Had they just seen this creature, this thing that they didn't understand, and made up a story to explain it?

Brobson had already come upon the spot where trees fall in the woods with nobody around to hear, and now he'd met the tree himself.

"I was praying," Brobson told Doering.

The doctor accepted this, because he had to.

THIRTY-EIGHT

OERING REQUISITIONED A sandwich from one of the other searchers. Brobson had no idea what was on it when he took that first heavenly bite, nor did he have a clue what he'd just eaten after the last. What he savored wasn't its taste, but its essence. Never before had he fully appreciated the luxury of being able to eat whenever he pleased.

It was humbling to think that he'd only gone a little over a day without food. What a life of plenty he'd led.

But this wasn't to say he didn't have any problems of his own. He most certainly did, the most pressing of which was how to get out of this camp-within-a-camp.

It was going to be much easier said than done: there were only four tents for just under twenty people, and these were not big tents. Except, of course, for the Reverend Doctor's. So that was where Brobson was stuck, along with Doering, Rowan and two other guys who must have been head honchos in their own shrunken-head ways. Malamar, surprisingly, had no issue with this – he was only too happy to personally ensure the prodigal son's return.

Hal was in a different tent. Brobson would probably not get to say goodbye to him. He hoped a successful escape would express his gratitude in full.

The rain began with a cute little *drip drip* committee. Then a solid sheet of water came crashing down, as though the planet Earth had just bellyflopped into a celestial sea. The roof of the tent buckled slightly but held. The heavens filled the polyester depression with a liquid drumroll.

Brobson's plan was to crawl into the sleeping bag that Doering had brought for him, close his eyes, and pretend to be asleep. There was no other first move to make; he'd been stuffed into the back of the tent, with five full-grown men between him and the zipperflap. The quarters were close – it would be a challenge to tiptoe between their sleeping bodies, but he felt he could do it. Only as long as they were sleeping though, lights out, three-Z's, deep in a dream *asleep*. Somebody in even a twilight state would hear him, and very likely feel Brobson's foot brushing against their shoulder as he Twistered his way out. And there was no way anybody would be conking out if they thought he was still awake. So he needed to pretend, and make it look good.

Well, he certainly did.

How long had he been asleep? It was still dark, so dark he had trouble seeing what the others in the tent were up to. Lo and behold, the friendly lightning bugs had called in their supervisor: lightning cracked the sky like a walnut, giving Brobson an instant to assess the tent.

He counted five shadows on the floor, still, but somehow coiled.

Could it be that easy? Were they all asleep? There was a chance that some had been disturbed by the lightning. That would incline him towards waiting a few minutes, but time was not on his side. This sleeping bag was too cozy, and he was too tired. He couldn't risk falling asleep again.

Time passed differently when he was alone in the woods, but here, swaddled in civilization, it was inescapable, inexorable. One minute, two, three, Brobson was painfully aware of every second ticking by. Sometimes the night would try to lull him back to sleep with its thunderous flatulence, but Brobson refused.

When he could take it no longer, he made the call. It was now or never. He would just have to trust that the five Men in the tent were all asleep, and if they weren't, he would have to hope that a full belly, battery of painkillers and spot of sleep would carry him beyond their reaching arms and into the loving tempest.

Slowly, pursing his lips to hold back the gasp of pain his entire body was so eager to hear, he pulled his left leg out of the sleeping bag. First the thigh. Then the knee. The calf. The bum ankle. The toes.

He stretched the leg out, and just as slowly let out his breath. He drew another and began the liberation of the right.

Another flashbulb from heaven lit the tent.

One of the shadows was sitting bolt upright.

Darkness again. Brobson tried to listen for movement, some sign of wakefulness, but the splatter on the canvas was deafening.

So he did all he could do: he resumed retrieval of his right leg, eyes locked on the space where the shadow had been. It was only two people away, its head on the side of the tent where Brobson had his feet.

He longed for the days when he could imagine that shadows were fantastical creatures from a fairy tale. Oh, what he would not have given to be fretting over Finchley right now.

The thigh. The knee. The ca-

"Stop," the shadow commanded in the Reverend Doctor Keith Malamar's voice.

THIRTY-NINE

ANOTHER FLASH N' crash revealed the Reverend Doctor tiptoeing his way over Doering, who had made a point of lying between them. Brobson instinctively pulled back his legs to allow room for God, or at least His hype man.

Brobson's upper lip and nose began to pulse, a weak warmth too timid to stick around.

It was Malamar's breath. Brobson didn't need a flash of recognition to know. He could feel the intrusion into his personal space, the tug of the sleeping bag as new weight was added to the tail.

"I need to make something very clear to you," Malamar whispered, his voice like a shovel dragged across concrete. Whoever this was, it was not the Reverend Doctor Keith Malamar who went on TV.

Brobson said nothing to this. He knew Malamar would be expounding upon this 'something' regardless

235

of Brobson's response. He also had a pretty good idea that it wasn't going to be anything he wanted to hear: if it weren't bad news, Malamar probably wouldn't be whispering. He didn't strike Brobson as the kind of guy who grasped the concept of "Don't Wake Daddy".

Mercifully, the throbbing of breath on Brobson's face receded. He still couldn't hear anything over the rain, but he felt the sleeping bag tug a little bit more beneath him. Malamar was settling down at the other end of it.

Another blast of lightning confirmed this. Brobson and Malamar now sat facing each other, the former with his knees bent and tucked into his chest, the latter cross-legged. It was a peaceful posture marred by a terrifying visage; the Reverend Doctor was like a zen master who'd just sat on his balls.

"I was supposed to be in my suite at the Mokara tonight. Best hotel in Texas. Best hotel in the whole God-fearing state of Texas. And I had the *very best room* in the best hotel in the whole state of Texas. Top floor. Great big bed. A big, *soft* bed, with one of those duvets that are *heavy*, because they're so fucking comfortable. Oh! And a river view, too. I was going to watch the sun rise over the, the…whatever they call their little river, with a stiff drink in my hand, that they were going to *bring to my door*. But then *no*, first I had to put in an appearance *here*. Well, at the thing. Whatever. Do that little speech for you weirdos. Like you even care who's fluffing up the party line, right? Oooh, AIDS blood, oooooh, uh… whatever, you know? But apparently I have to because, what, I guess I own this fucking place? That's what they told me. I don't even remember buying it, but…I guess I did! Must have been useful at some point. Who can remember? Anyway, I show up here, I do the gig. Next flight to Texas, everything's fine. I've still got a week to wile away, do a few sermons here and there. Plenty of megachurches in Texas. None as big as mine, if we're counting podcast listeners and Facebook followers in the congregation, and why not, I say. Still counts. They're still hearing the Word. Th-"

"Mr. Malamar?" Brobson interrupted. He knew this would be rewarded with more rage, but he was getting restless. Every moment spent listening to this diatribe was a moment closer to morning, and so to the irreversible sealing of his fate. "I'm confused."

"Reverend Doctor," Malamar corrected sharply. "And I'm painting you a picture, so you can fully appreciate how…*inconvenient* you are. So you can appreciate how unpleasant it is for me to be *here*, in a dirty tent, in the pouring rain, with three wackos and a queer."

The sleeping bag shifted again, but Brobson couldn't see where Malamar was moving to. A little light on the situation would have been nice. Just a quick flash.

"Now I'm paying for a five-star, well, four-and-a-half, this *is* Texas we're talking about, a four-and-a-half star hotel room, I'm paying for that and *I'm not in it*. Absolute waste of collection offerings. Not to mention, I'm going to be *not getting paid* for at *least* the first speaking gig, and I'll be lucky if I can sweet-talk them into not pursuing a breach of contract fee. But, either way, that's a relationship strained, and let me tell you, mine is a *business* of relationships. Statewide, local, national, even international sometimes. It's all connected."

"What about your relationship to God?" Brobson asked, trying to disguise the cheek in piety, which to him had always put him in mind of someone frantically making a balloon animal while watching a small hourglass.

Malamar said nothing to this. The rain did the talking. It didn't have much to say, and it was so excited to say it.

"What we have here," he finally resumed, "is an optics problem. It's a toxic narrative. That's the problem. If it were just a rotten story, that'd be one thing. Let Rowan take the blame, close the camp. I couldn't care less. But it's not just rotten. It's *toxic*. So we have to change the narrative. How would you like to help me do that?"

Brobson assumed that this was a question with a built-in answer. He assumed correctly.

"I was up trying to mull this over. You made a hell of a racket getting out of that bag, I'll tell you. It's a wonder you escaped the first time. Couldn't afford a marching band to follow you out?" Malamar chuckled at that. He liked it a lot. "Two heads are better than one though, even if the one on your shoulders is small and soft. So let's work through this. Some options. Option one is you die."

Of course there was simultaneous tumult of thunder and lightning just then. Malamar also seemed to appre-

238

ciate the supreme perfection of the moment: Brobson saw a toothy smile plastered across his face.

He hoped Malamar couldn't feel him shivering through the sleeping bag.

"You die from your infection. I'm not suggesting that I would *kill* you, *please*," he pleaded in a tone of voice that made clear he wanted Brobson to intuit precisely that, "I'm just saying, you die, we throw you in a ditch or something, go on our way. I get everybody to keep quiet, throw them some money and a copy of the NDAs they fucking better have signed. We go back and say we couldn't find you. Now you're just a moody kid who ran away and we're the heroes who bent over backwards to track you down. And then they feel bad for *us* that we couldn't! That'd play well in Texas – I could reschedule the whole tour at a higher fee, I bet. Point is, no reporters can come ask for your take on things. That one's got some holes, but it's neat. I like it.

"Doering's got you on the mend, though, and he says you'll probably be fine as long as we get you some antibiotics. So I can't hold my breath on that one. So we move on t-"

"Mr. Reverend Doctor?"

"No 'Mr.' – What?"

"I don't really understand…why would people care that much if I die?"

Rain. Lightning. Thunder. "I honestly have no idea. I've *met* you and I wouldn't care. I think it's just because you're a kid. And the gay camp thing's pretty hot button. Your parents aren't connected, are they?"

239

Brobson imagined Mom and Dad conjoined at the hip. That probably wasn't what he meant. "To what?"

"Politics, sports, entertainment, whatever. I assume they're not. I'd have known."

"No, but, I mean, why would anybody care if I got hurt or died? The government has been executing the gay kids, and s-"

Malamar laughed once, loudly. Brobson heard a fleshy *slap*, presumably the Reverend Doctor clapping a hand over his own mouth. After a few quickly-swallowed chuckles, and a mumbled something or other about not waking the wackos, Malamar reemerged. *"What?"*

That was not the reaction Brobson had anticipated. "They...everybody said that, *you* said, that because we have AIDS in our bl-"

"Oh, I know. I just can't...you still *believe* all that? I figured you ran away because you were over it. You left even though you imagined your own government was killing all the queers? Where did you think you were going?"

Brobson hung his head. But he didn't answer the question. Because, in a flash of a wholly different kind, he suddenly saw a way that he might still get to Aunt Matilda's.

"I don't know," Brobson replied. "I just wanted to get away. I didn't want to get hit anymore." He slowly reached into his right pocket, well aware that a sudden movement might unnerve Malamar. Then again, that could be an overly generous reading on the man's situational awareness.

240

"Yeah, I heard about that. He got you good with a belt buckle, huh? Probably cried about it after. Him, not you. Rowan's funny that way."

For a moment, Brobson couldn't find it. The pit of his stomach dropped – and then bungeed back up. Turned out he'd just forgotten how deep his pockets were. He found the arrowhead, plucked from the river-bed. He'd known it would come in handy. Thanks, clumsy Native American guy from a bazillion years ago.

He turned it so the smooth sides were perpendicular to his palm.

It was his turn to talk. He had to say something else before the next step. He wasn't sure he wouldn't make some noises as it happened – better to have Malamar talking, then, just in case.

"*I* didn't cry after," was all Brobson could think to say. He couldn't even remember if that was true or not. It had happened so long ago.

"That doesn't surprise me, actually."

"So I don't have AIDS?"

"I mean, anything's possible. I don't know your life."

And then Malamar kept talking, but Brobson stopped listening. Instead he dug the point of the arrowhead into the meat of his palm and squeezed, as hard as he could.

He was really hoping, between the miseries he'd experienced in the woods and the painkillers he'd received just a few hours ago, that this wouldn't hurt all that much. He was disappointed.

But not for long – he felt the blood course out of his

241

palm, dribbling off the arrowhead and pooling at the bottom of his pocket.

Through the pain, he smiled. He never thought he would do that again.

In the next flash of lightning, Malamar must have seen Brobson's face. He stopped talking in the middle of a word, and said "What."

Through the hungry dark, Brobson lunged, leading with his right palm, hoping that Malamar hadn't moved since the light had died.

He hadn't. Brobson felt his bloody hand *splat* right onto a surprisingly leathery face.

Fighting nine years of Ten Commandment-bred deference, he smeared his palm around the Reverend's moneymaker, coating Malamar's eyes, nose and mouth with as much substance as a small life could muster.

"FUCKER!" Malamar sputtered. He popped Brobson on the jaw and shoved him back with a kick from his once-shiny shoes.

Brobson thumped against the far wall of the tent. The two of them had made quite a ruckus. He hoped someone heard it over the rain. If not, well, he could make himself heard.

What he could hear now was Malamar spitting and wiping his face. "God! What the fuck? Is this your blood?!"

"Yes," Brobson proudly informed him. "It's my gay AIDS blood."

"I…have you been listening to a goddamned word I just said?"

"Yes. You don't believe I have AIDS."

"You *don't*."

"So *you* don't believe it." Brobson gestured towards three sleeping beauties in the tent, hoping the lightning would trace his outstretched arm for Malamar. It didn't, but that was alright. "What about them?"

For a moment, it was just Brobson and Malamar, listening to the rain poking at the tent, wishing desperately it had a point, that it hadn't come all this way to just burst and vanish.

"Oh," Malamar said, "that's not fair."

Brobson screamed.

FORTY

"**A**IDS BLOOD! MY AIDS BLOOD!"
Brobson shrieked over the pounding rain,
hoisting himself to his feet as he did.

Doering, the nearest shadow to them, was the first
to respond. "What is it?" he asked, with remarkable
lucidity.

"MY AIDS BLOOD," Brobson explained.

"It's nothing!" Malamar shouted somewhere between the rain and Brobson. "He's having a nigh-"

The sun crashed into the tent like a wrecking ball,
pinning Brobson and Malamar to the far wall of canvas
like fingerpaintings on a fridge.

A flashlight. Somebody here was quick with the
flashlight. Brobson had been counting on a moment of
shock to make his escape – he would need to be faster
than he'd expected.

He shot a quick look towards Malamar, just to ens-

245

ure his face was as grisly as Brobson had hoped. It was; the Reverend Doctor was a pair of blinking white eyes beneath a thick smear of Brobson's handmade tomato puree.

Brobson shifted the arrowhead to the left pocket.

"Saints alive!" cried one of the two guys Brobson had never seen before.

"Keith!" Rowan's voice cracked as he called his boss' name.

Brobson held his awkward squatting position. He couldn't move with the light trained on him. He needed that light *off*, or pointed away from him. He needed the night.

Uncertain of how to escalate the situation beyond this, Brobson settled for a trick he learned from Reverend Malamar – strenuous repetition. "He ate some of my blood! It's gay and there's AIDS in it," he reminded them.

And then everything happened.

In a single instant:

Malamar took a half-hearted swipe at Brobson and insisted "no there *isn't!*"

Doering started to say "Actually, th-" but that was as far as he got because:

Rowan HOWLED like First Stone's siren, a wretched ululation that started baritone, slid up to tenor, then shot straight up to a falsetto.

One of the other two guys in the tent said "here!"

And then Rowan slapped aside the light in his dash towards Malamar. Brobson caught a flash of starchy

246

white handkerchief.

He saw, and felt, more bodies converging on the Reverend.

"NO!" Malamar shouted as Brobson dove through the crush. "GET OFF OF ME!"

"Sorry," Brobson mumbled to the flashlight-wielding Doering as he karate chopped the good doctor's armpit. As Doering winced and recoiled, he dropped the flashlight – right into Brobson's waiting hand.

Ouch. So the cut might have been pretty deep after all.

"IT MIGHT NOT BE TOO LATE!" Rowan shrieked to Malamar. "WE CAN SAVE YOU!"

"NOT ME!" The Doctor snarled at his would-be rescuers. "GRAB THE FAGGOT!"

Brobson popped out of the tent like a baby tooth tied to a slamming door. The campsite was coming alive, each of the tents illuminated from within, host to languid, molten shadows, alien lava lamps on a hostile planet.

Even through the storm, Brobson could hear flaps unzipping. He knew only too well that nobody here came in peace.

He clicked off his flashlight and barreled out of the loose circle of camp. Just as he reached the treeline, a celestial flashbulb popped and revealed a loose pile of bags.

Supplies.

Brobson snatched one up as he fled the gathering voices, hurtling blindly into the familiar wilderness. He screamed as he ran, hoping desperately that the storm would conceal his cries.

He felt everything. The infected wound on his back, his rolled ankle, his shredded leg, his sliced wrist, the xylophone solo in his ribs, the pounding of his head, the clenching of his heart, the itching and peeling of his skin, and every little bump and bruise and bugbite he'd picked up in between. Adrenaline had forsaken him, as had everything and everyone else. He felt it all.

He was going to be goddamned if this was for nothing.

FORTY-ONE

H E STOPPED WHEN the only alternative was collapse.

The rain held steady, but fortunately the lightning had picked up. It allowed him to progress at pace using scattered glimpses of the path he was slicing through the dark. In fact, he got quite good at taking in as much information as possible from his little split-second premonitions. He still slipped and tripped plenty. But certainly not as much as he could have.

The only worthwhile way to think about time right now was endurance, and he was at the ass end of his. So he plopped onto a rock, listened as hard as he could to the night, and rolled the dice. He clicked on the flashlight.

Shadows dove out of the way, hiding behind rocks and trees. Brobson couldn't blame them. He'd be doing the same thing.

He trained the beam on the knapsack he'd picked

up. It was a boring lumpy green drawstring thing, like somebody had stuck a bicycle pump into a pea and gone to town. But boring-looking things were so often the most useful.

By and large, this one wasn't.

Some of the stuff inside – a diary, a pair of headphones, hand sanitizer – he discarded out of hand, flinging them beyond his spotlight. Others, like a half-full canteen (he'd let the rainwater refill it later) and a first aid kit, he put to one side while he finished exhuming the remaining contents of the bag.

Two things he stuffed directly into his pockets. The first was a granola bar. It was one of those nasty crunchy ones, and it had raspberries. But these were desperate times.

The second was a small silver lighter.

A lighter nearly identical to the stolen one that Fischer had shown him, once upon a time.

Brobson held it in his hands, watching how the flashlight's beam danced on its brassy contours and wished it could be more elemental, like what lived inside.

It reminded him of a different time. Not simpler. Just one when complexities didn't have to be contradictions.

He wanted, more than anything, to flip the lighter open, click the wheel, and stare at the flame. But he knew it would never catch in a place like this.

Brobson put it in his pocket for later.

He clicked off his flashlight and picked up the canteen, unscrewing the lid to…

…

He could still see the canteen. Dimly, but he could.

Turning on one knee, he looked behind him. Spears of light waved from between the trees. Raindrops lunged through the space between Brobson and his pursuers, like a million Secret Service agents hoping to catch a bullet.

"LEAVE ME ALONE!" he wailed, not at all of his own accord. He had no idea how they'd followed him, but there was no point asking.

Oh. The flashlight. Duh.

Well, at this stage, no point crashing around in the dark. He clicked on his flashlight and followed the beam.

FORTY-TWO

THEY WERE GAINING on him. He could make out voices, furious, distant. Not distant enough.

It was impossible to run *and* keep the beam of the flashlight level and steady. He was creating little lightning strikes between the real ones, a strobe of muddled foresight. The metronomic quality of it was hypnotic. Brobson was scarcely aware of what he was doing, or why he was doing it. He just *was*. He wondered if he always would be.

The forest stretched ever onward, the night by its side.

FORTY-THREE

THE TREES BECKONED, their rain-tasseled boughs guiding him home. Come to me, each one said. You are home.

Brobson felt like he was running around the inside of a wheel. Up was down, down was left, right just wasn't. His legs kept pumping, yet his strides grew crooked and shallow. Somehow his left ankle had caught on fire. Or been stabbed. It was beyond a roll. So much worse. An unbroken scream was beyond his grasp; after each lung-crushing breath, he wheezed out a roar to push himself through. He could barely even hear them. This would not be enough.

He wasn't home. He didn't want to be home. He wanted to be somewhere better. Needed to be.

FORTY-FOUR

THE DELUGE PARTED its jaws. Its maw was impossible to miss. It was the darkest thing in the world.

Brobson had seen this before. He'd passed it by. That was where Finchley Shivers lived. That was what he'd believed. Look how that worked out.

Finchley Shivers wasn't real. But the Reverend Doctor Keith Malamar was. But AIDS blood wasn't. But First Stone was. But sin wasn't, couldn't be. But pain was. Would be.

What might be found in the root-rimmed well of the oak was uncertain. Maybe it was no deeper than its own shadow. Maybe it was full of water. Maybe it was a way out, as it had been for Finchley. To enter was to forfeit the certainties of which he'd always been assured. But all he could be assured of were hurt and humiliation. Certainty was the end. Uncertainty...

Brobson threw his flashlight as far away as he could and dove head first into the underworld.

FORTY-FIVE

HE DIDN'T GET far.

Luckily, he hadn't immediately hit his head on the inside of the tree. He was *under* it. He could feel roothair tickling the back of his neck. There was barely enough space for him to fit. Yet he had.

Mostly.

What had caught?

Craning his head back, he saw. The bag of supplies. It was too big to follow him into the hole.

He'd slung the drawstring across his chest like a bandolier. Unslinging it in such a narrow space might be impossible. Going back outside was the only option.

That was possible, but barely. He wriggled and scooted back out, feet first. He imagined it looked like the tree was birthing him. He hoped nobody else was seeing it clear enough to confirm.

When his head was out, he ripped the bag off his

259

head and slid it away. As he plunged himself back into the darkness, he felt a hand grasp his ankle. Not his good ankle.

So the flashlight decoy fake-out hadn't worked either.

He screamed and kicked at the hand. On second thought, maybe it was fortunate his good ankle had been left free. The grasping hand gripped tighter. Brobson kicked and kicked until his good ankle became a second bad ankle.

That did it.

Free from hangers-on, Brobson slithered deeper into the space between the tree and the earth. The soil beneath his chest was soggy, yielding. The woodwork above him had greater conviction.

From behind him, shouts. Scrabbling sounds. Finally, light.

Brobson hoped they got a real nice look at the soles of his shoes. Two soles and a soul they couldn't save.

The harsh white flood poured into a place it had no business being. Brobson could see patches of his route. To the right and left. Directly in front of him remained a mystery, blotted out by his own shadow.

More shouting. Brobson wasn't listening. He just kept crawling.

The tree finally gave up. Yielded. Turned out the soil was the more tenacious of the two.

Brobson crawled through a tunnel of dirt. Then he started sliding. It was arcing downwards. Down meant Hell. Down meant the Fall.

Down meant freedom.

A bottom-up curtain closed out the light show. The voices faded away.

Brobson crawled deeper and deeper. The passage grew narrower on all sides. Closing in. He grunted with each thrusting arm. Each kicking leg.

Pressure on his back, on his stomach. His chest couldn't fully expand. His breaths were shallow, getting shallower. Gulps became sips. His lungs could hold no more.

His elbows hit the sides of the wall. He bashed his knee trying to reposition.

The tunnel was too narrow for his head. The only way forward was to turn it to one side, half-bury his noggin in the soft dirt. So he did.

It was hard to keep going. He'd burrowed his head in up to almost the nose-side of his left eye. His fully submerged ear brought him the sound of his own heartbeat. b-Bum b-Bum b-Bum. It was too fast.

Clawing at the soil, he plowed forward.

His arms were useless. Elbows bent, they were pinned to his chest, his hands just beneath his chin.

Brobson pushed himself further. Shimmying with his shoulders. Pressing with his toes. Inch by inch.

The ceiling of the burrow dipped further still. Before long it was touching the top of Brobson's head.

With his next inch forward, it pressed.

The further he went, the more the Earth drove his face downward, and accepted it. Face, Earth. One and the same.

261

When Brobson had sacrificed half of his head to his hungry host, he stopped. Any further would see his second nostril claimed like the first. He couldn't open his mouth at all.

He couldn't go any further.

But his arms were pinned. His head was too. He couldn't bend his knees.

Sucking oxygen through his lone exposed nostril as powerfully as he could, Brobson dug his toes into the dirt. Tried to pull himself back.

Tried again.

And again.

And again.

He couldn't do it.

He was stuck.

FORTY-SIX

H E IMAGINED HIMSELF dying down here. It wasn't hard to do. Malamar would get his wish, and Brobson would have done him the favor of burying himself.

How far beneath the ground was he? What had he expected to find down here?

No. He had known this was a possibility. He had accepted it as a risk worth taking. There was no point second-guessing it.

Still, he began to cry. He was terrified. This was it. Couldn't be helped.

He sniffed through his one remaining nostril, wet and heavy.

His runny eye bulged, spilling his horror into the soil.

If he kept crying, his nostril might clog up.

He could cry himself dead.

Or he could keep going.

263

And he could hope.
He breathed deep.
Barely a breath.
Maybe enough.
To keep going.
He had to go.
Bowed head.
Not praying.
Struggling.
Different.
Better.
Hard.
Dig.
Go.
In.
A.
I.

.

FORTY-SEVEN

BROBSON KNEW THAT he could hold his breath for forty-five seconds. That, he had always been told, was terrifically impressive.

There was no way he was only under the dirt for forty-five seconds.

Eons passed, during which he pushed himself deeper, further, lower. Civilizations rose and fell as he bored his way into their bedrock. They never knew.

And yet, he kept going. On a single, one-nostril breath, he dug himself deeper. All those people who talked about rock bottom? They had no idea. All they'd have had to do was dig. They'd have seen. The bottom is only where you put it. You can always go deeper.

You just have to want it.

Brobson wanted i-

Something was happening.

265

His cocoon was splitting.

He felt the dirt beneath his stomach g-

Oh no, i-

WHA-

"AAAAAAAAAAAAAAAH!" said Brobson, with a brand new drought of fresh air to power his cry.

The entire world, sick and tired of holding him up, slid away. But it pulled him along for one last ride, yanking his shirt up past his belly button as it did.

He plummeted through the darkness. And then he learned that he, too, had a rock bottom. It had been waiting for him, since the dawn of time. Buried. Silent. Blind. Patient.

Brobson hit it hard and called it a motherfucker.

FORTY-EIGHT

H E WAS...SOMEWHERE. Or maybe not. Maybe he'd died. If so, everybody who fancied they knew what to expect from the hereafter was in for an unpleasant surprise.

Black. Pitch black. All black everything.

But he could still feel his body. He told it to stand. Countless passions testified to his success. He was pushing himself to his feet. Every single joint in his body cracked, like the world's worst improv troupe.

Closing his eyes as though it made a difference, he sucked in air, his chest expanding to three times its normal size. He had eighteen lungs. He had never had so much air in his body at once. It was magnificent.

He leaned backwards, stretching out his spine. Who knew simply throwing your arms over your head could feel so good? Perhaps his true calling was as a football points zebra. A ref! Suddenly the appeal of that thank-

267

less profession made sense.

But first thing was, invariably, first. Before he could officiate the Super Bowl, he had to find a way out of whatever underground chamber he'd fallen in to.

If only he could see.

Chuckling to himself – he would have laughed, but his body could only meet mirth halfway – he pulled the lighter out of his pocket. He'd pocketed it not because it would have done him any good in the deluge, but because it was what Fischer had pocketed ages ago. It made him think of Fischer. Because, yeah, he liked Fischer. Not just as a friend, not just as a pal. As a Valentine too. Brobson loved Fischer. They were both boys and he loved him *and* liked him and it didn't matter, especially down here. Especially down here, it was the only thing that mattered. It was the only way to see in the dark.

He flipped back the lid and clicked the wheel.

Nothing happened.

Brobson frowned and clicked it again.

A single spark winked.

It illuminated a human face.

Brobson fumbled the lighter. He snagged it in mid-air. Clicked the wheel a third time.

The flame grew up so fast, beginning life as a small blue orb in the brass cradle of the lighter. Almost immediately it went through bluberty, growing to three times its original size, developing into a complex gradient of yellow, orange and red, without violating its essential blue-ness.

268

As the light gained confidence, it traced Brobson's predicament. The hole in the ceiling about ten feet up told him he'd fallen through a thin patch of dirt and landed in this underground chamber. It was ovular, with eerily neat walls. There were patterns in the well-packed dirt, like terraces on an ancient temple.

There was also a person in the chamber with him, which rather distracted from the wallpaper.

Not a person.

A fantasy.

Finchley Shivers.

"You're not real," Brobson informed him.

Finchley growled, his face rearranging like a hustler's cups. Watch the ball, find the lady.

It wasn't a game worth playing. Brobson was already playing out a hand towards much higher stakes.

The figment of Brobson's imagination turned and knuckled along the perimeter of the cavern. It rumbled and grumbled all the while. A monologue.

Brobson turned his back on Finchley and drew his flame closer to the walls of the chamber. He raked his fingers through the tightly packed dirt, barely tilling enough to soil his fingernails.

Like breaching whales, words burst from the depths of Finchley's nonsense, and vanished just as quickly. The first one that Brobson understood was "me". That was always the way with dreadful fantasies. Me, me, me.

Some of the others, which Brobson tried and failed to ignore as he mirrored Finchley's circumnavigation, were "blood", "name", "trade", "father" and "moon".

Brobson completed his round, finding no promising means of escape. He lowered himself to the ground to consider his options. The flame in his hand flickered. Right. These things couldn't run forever.

He blew out the flame and gently flipped the lid down.

That didn't look right. That wasn't what Fischer had done.

Brobson reopened the lid and flicked the wheel with his thumb. The flame reappeared.

Finchley was standing directly above Brobson, his long arms spread and planted in the dirt, halfway up Brobson's calves. "My story," the creature began in unbroken English, "tells of how I came to be th-"

"There's lots of stories that aren't true," Brobson replied. He flicked his hand, quick and short. The lid of the lighter *kchunk*ed shut of its own accord. Darkness. Yeah, that was it.

Brobson flicked it the other way. He heard the metallic *kchink* of the lid flipping open. He struck the wheel. *Fft*, the flame was back.

He was alone. Just him and the flame. But only when he needed it. This wasn't compulsory company. It never wore out its welcome.

kchunk

...

kchink

fft

...

kchunk

270

...

kchink

fft

...

kchunk

...

FORTY-NINE

H E SAT IN the dark.

It was a new experience. Strangely pleasant. For the first time in his life, there was no punishment on the horizon.

It wasn't until he'd acclimatized to solitude that he heard it. A sound, wet and unambitious, like butter drizzling on popcorn. So quiet it could well have been silence that had gotten confused for a second. But there it was and there it remained. *Thlhlhlhlhl.*

kchink

fft

Brobson looked around at the earthen dome. Not only could he not see anything – with the light on, he couldn't even hear the sound anymore. His jealous eyes had resumed captaincy.

They would just see about that. Ha, ha.

He surveyed his approximate position in the pit,

committed it to memory as best he could, and *kchunk*ed himself into mutinous black.

The sound was gone. But Brobson knew better than to panic.

A few minutes later it was back. *Thlhlhlhhl.*

Moving slowly, to minimize both the deafening roar of his shuffling feet, as well as the probability of his tripping on the incline of the wall and taking a fall, Brobson followed the sound as best he could. He stuck a hand out to anchor himself along the wall, but the skittering of his fingers along the dirt drowned out the sound.

Thlhlhlhl.

He was getting closer.

His toe met the ground faster than he'd expected. "Guh," he woofed. He regained his balance and resumed the hunt.

Thlhlhlhl.

Even closer.

Thlhlhlhl.

He was moving away from it.

It was somewhere on the stretch of wall he'd just passed.

Backtracking and doubling back again in ever decreasing oscillations, he homed in on the source.

Through the blind pitch, he extended his hand until he felt the wall.

It was damp. Much more so than the other sections of wall he'd touched.

Whatever it was, this was it.

274

kchink

fft

This portion of the hollow looked identical to the others. It was why he'd walked right past it. But there was indisputably something different about it.

Just beneath the skin, easily punctured with a tightly clawed hand, the Earth here was muddy. Even more so than what Brobson had burrowed through in the tunnel above. He scooped out a handful. It could hardly wait to get out of there, plopping enthusiastically to the ground.

At long last, Brobson and the world were in complete agreement.

Every fiber of his being screamed *DIG*, but there was no way of knowing how long this would take, or where it would lead him. Perhaps to another cavern. He could be digging for days.

He sat down, took a deep breath, and reached into his pocket. Brobson peeled off the wrapper and attacked the granola bar as carefully as he would the sodden wall. Just as soon as he was finished with the bar. Had raspberries ever tasted so good? Which was to say, good?

THE LIGHTER TOOK up residence on the ground, just to the right of Brobson's intended work zone. He scooped the dirt out primarily with his left hand, as the self-slashed stigmata of the right hurt too much to help. It was slow going, with each extraction being celebrated by some new party favor from the planet. Usually it was an increasingly large squirt of water, which Brobson tried and failed to drink an embarrassing number of times. Sometimes it was a small collapse, or a mini-mudslide. Once it was a not-so-mini-mudslide; on that occasion, Brobson dashed to the other end of the pit, fearing he would be swallowed and entombed. Such was the fate of his lighter. He spent fifteen minutes searching for it. Time and energy wasted. Stumbling his way back into his excavation, he resumed shifting mud by the fistful, by committing to memory what the light had taught him.

Once again, he kept himself sane by keeping time. He discovered that aligning his movements to the passing seconds could power him through his slumps.

It took him about seven seconds to complete one scoop. Seconds one and two were for removing the mud. Three through five were tossing the dirt back out into the chamber. Six and seven saw his hand returning to first position. When he counted fourteen, he ought to have done two scoops since he started counting. Twenty-eight would be four. And so on.

As he dug for his life, he also finally learned a times table.

THREE THOUSAND, THREE hundred and fifty five scoops. Brobson counted every single one. Three thousand, three hundred and fifty *six* scoops. He hadn't missed a single seven-count, hadn't paused or rested. Sweat had poured into his eyes, stinging them shut. That was fine. He wasn't using them. Three thousand, three hundred and fifty *seven*. What kept him going was the feeling of progress. Imagined or not, it seemed as though the mud grew softer, simpler to move with each scoop. All three thousand, three hundred and fifty *eight* scoops. Whether that meant he was moving towards a new life or a slow death was impossible to know. All that mattered was he was moving towards *something*, moving forward. Three thousand, three hundred and fifty *nope*.

In trying to fetch the next load, Brobson triggered another mini-mudslide. Except instead of making a long squish sound, it made a bunch of smaller splats.

It was hard to hear the splats, though. Over the din of a forest at daybreak.

FIFTY

EVERY PART OF Brobson's body went rogue at once. His right arm punched his lolling head in its grimacing face, grinding the sweat out of his eyes. His left arm flailed out at the lip of his hard-won egress. His legs hustled him out into the world. He peed a little bit. He felt he was entitled. It had been a long couple of days.

Parting his eyelids little by little, Brobson took in his surroundings. His own tunnel had deposited him into a *much* larger one, at least two stories tall and just as wide. There was a load of junk on the floor, dirty buckets and heavy ropes and rusty shovels all thrown willy-nilly. If there had been a snowblower tucked in the back, he'd have said he'd found the much-feared bear's garage.

To his left, the tunnel ventured off to look for something in the dark. To his right, just some twenty-five feet from where he'd emerged, it had already found the

279

morning. Sunlight scattered in the after-rain mists. It was an eager dawn, a birthday boy who couldn't decide which present to open first.

Standing between Brobson and the world reborn were five demons perched on a mountain of coal.

They'd carved hard-edged fractals into their faces, and poured into them the extremities of the tunnel they guarded. Pale grey eyes fused the darkness and the light, projecting only the worst of both. Their heads were shrouded in thick, wild manes; their bodies, adorned with studded, spiked armor. Each held an instrument of torment. Each embodied the knowledge of its application.

This couldn't be. Demons weren't real. Finchley had been a demon. Finchley wasn't real. He had vanished. He was a demon. He wasn't real. Demons couldn't be real.

Not after everything he'd been through.

"YOU'RE NOT REAL!" Brobson screamed at the hellions. He was aware of falling. And then he was back in the tunnel. Digging. Digging. Digging.

FIFTY-ONE

THE NEPHROTIC SYNDROME, Brobson would later learn, was a death metal band from Philipsburg. Its founding members were two inseparable chums named Gale Widgery (rhythm guitar, vocals) and Clifton Saltonstall (lead guitar), who'd stuck together from second grade all the way to a local community college, from which they graduated with degrees in Business Administration and Finance, respectively.

That was how they made a living. How they *lived* was through music, specifically the kind that made perfectly reasonable folks want to start using each other as a jungle gym.

Metal wasn't about aggression or anger to Gale and Clifton. Well, not entirely. It was about having an opportunity to simultaneously release and embrace life's

281

endless complications. It was also really fun to climb around on people – there were so few socially acceptable opportunities to do that.

This sort of dual thinking was what led Gale and Clifton to create Nils and Bontz. Embodying an alter-ego on stage, with makeup and costumes and a little backstory, the whole nine yards – this was a way of celebrating absurdity in more than just music. It was also a really handy gimmick to get people to their concerts, which was invaluable in a glutted market.

So Gale and Clifton found a bassist, a drummer and a keyboardist (no modern death metal band should leave home without one) who were as excited by the gag as they were. They applied, critiqued and tweaked their corpsepaint until it was just right. Clifton trawled yard sales for ratty old sports gear and animal pelts he could turn into an iconic getup. Gale hammered out a history for the band, heavy on Satanic conquests and barbarian iconography. He did not mention his Bachelor's degree.

Much to the dismay of their old academic advisors, Gale Widgery became Nils Grunforce (blackcoat bishop, extracting obeisance to the Father of Lies), while Clifton Saltonstall morphed into Bontz Numscrunt (conjuror, tormentor, Earth shaker).

Almost every single day, after long grinds in offices, Gale and Clifton would become themselves. Their bestudded gauntlets fit them better than starchy collared shirts, that was for sure.

The band wrote material, did some gigs, and got a

better reception than they'd expected. Only a year and change into the hustle, they were approached by a regionally recognized act, wondering if The Nephrotic Syndrome might not want to support them on a small East Coast tour.

All five members of the band said yes at exactly the same time.

The next day, they decided that it was time to get a website. And the first thing they needed was a picture to put on it.

But where to take the picture? It had to be somewhere *metal* but also not *too* metal, dark and disturbing without being distracting. A fake crime scene would be too much. A bus stop would be not enough.

After an Olympic afternoon on Google, drummer Greta Chandler (aka Deuteronomy Pfaffenbachen) turned up an abandoned bituminous coal mine about an hour and a half's drive away. It had looked awfully spooky in the photos. Lonely. Dismal. Brutal.

Metal.

After a nasty rainfall they made the call: it was photoshoot day. The idea behind shooting after rain was that the precipitation would help the mine breathe again, give it a disturbing, fleshy texture in the photo. It was a cute idea. So they got into costume, piled into the van, and drove.

The mouth of the mine was a bit of a hike, and some of them began to sweat their makeup off. They considered doing the shoot another day, but decided against it. They were already here. Easy enough to Photoshop out the smudges.

While they were at it, they might have to Photoshop *in* a few things. Like anything other than dirt and corroded gardening equipment. All eyes turned to Greta. She shrugged. The pictures she'd found online must have been old, and just as tantalizing to looters. The tracks and carts they'd been promised were nowhere to be found.

But still…they were already here. Might as well get the shot.

Gale set up his tripod and attached his camera, both of which he shared with his older brother and neither of which he really understood how to use. He'd had to look up how to use the timer feature online. Multiple times.

By now an old hand at it, Gale lined up the frame, directing his bandmates to stand a little bit higher on the pile of dirt, good, now tilt your head down, get some shadow from your forehead, perfect, now let's….

He dashed into the shot, assumed a grimacing touchdown posture that would have been an acceptable charade for 'man carrying five-foot halibut'. Brobson would have appreciated it.

The camera *click*ed.

Something behind them went *splat splat splat*.

As one, they all turned around.

The scorched, deformed corpse of a tiny coal miner punched its way out of an early grave. It had been waiting for them.

Mocking, it drew breath for which it had no use. Its

rattling gasps grew faster and faster, a timer ticking to zero.

Finally, it shrieked "YOU'RE NOT REAL!", and then plopped face-first into the dirt.

The Nephrotic Syndrome stared at the fallen child, waiting to see if he turned into a bat or, worse, identified himself as a YouTube prankster. Nobody wanted to be the first to say or do anything. It would invariably be the wrong thing.

Finally, bassist Ian Quaker (Gwimlin Al-Thormgrunch) whispered "brutal". That seemed about right.

They didn't say anything else until they'd gotten Brobson back down the mountain.

FIFTY-TWO

BROBSON AWOKE TO someone saying "he's awake!"

He opened his eyes slowly. Who was trespassing in his burrow?

There was light on the far side of his eyelids. They'd caught up with him. Beams speared him, not drawing blood. Tracing it, sketches to complete its own image.

He closed his eyes again. There was no light in the burrow. It wasn't allowed. The space beneath the forest was his. Not fair to take it. To make it visible, and so take it.

That wasn't right.

Wha?

He finished opening his eyes.

Trees slid past a smudged pane of glass. More trees than any human had probably ever seen in their entire lives, except Brobson. He'd seen them all before. It was like in movies, but probably not real life, when they line

287

the criminals up and ask the victim which one of these bad boys did the crime. There were big trees, little trees, fat trees, skinny trees, every kind of tree you could possibly think up – but all of them looked suspicious.

He knew their secrets, of course. Those which they had not revealed, he had discovered for himself. He knew which were innocent and which guilty. There was a difference.

He was on his way to First Stone. It had all been a dream, a nightmare, a fantasy that had whisked him away from the way back of Mom's Dodge Caravan as soon as he'd let his guard down.

No way Mom and Dad would send him to that place. No way.

And yet, Mom's Caravan looked different than it had when he'd first shut his eyes.

There were the monsters where there used to be seats. That was the most obvious difference. One monster driving, one monster in the passenger seat, three monsters in back. The ones up front were a boy monster and a girl monster, but they weren't married monsters – Brobson knew because they weren't Arguing About Directions.

No. Not monsters.

These were just five people who lived every day like it was Halloween.

"Wha…" Brobson gulped. He lay flat on his back, his head cradled in a grizzly bear's lap. Or shoulder. Or head. Who could tell – it was just a ball of fur now.

A young man slid over to Brobson. He'd wiped the

paint off of his face, but that was the extent of his un-dressing. Now he looked like one of those cardboard cutouts at a carnival, where you stick your face through a hole and it turns you into a farmer or an astronaut or whatever the hell these guys were supposed to be.

"It's okay," he informed Brobson as he pressed an almost-cool compress to his forehead, "you're safe. We're a death metal band."

"Well," the driver called over his shoulder, "our newer stuff actually draws more from black metal. *I* think."

"Too many melodies to call it black," another guy from the back rejoined.

"Well it's not *melodeath*."

"Honestly, it's closer to mathcore."

The woman in front turned around. "I'd call it a proggy synthesis of all our sounds thus far."

The driver raised a single finger. "With some djent!"

Everybody in the van said "NO."

Except the man kneeling over Brobson. He just closed his eyes, shook his head once, and found a smile. "My name's Gale." He waved a hand across his outfit. "I mention the band stuff to let you know we're not maniacs."

Brobson didn't need to be told. Real maniacs looked like everybody else.

Another guy scooted up, the only other one who'd remained quiet during the genre dispute. He had a phone in his hand. "We tried to call an ambulance, but there was no service. We're gonna try t-"

Rocketing up to a seated position as though yanked, Brobson shot an arm out towards the phone. "WAIT!"

The guy with the phone waited.

And so Brobson explained everything. Fischer. Valentine's Day. Mom and Dad. First Stone. His Buddies. Rowan. Malamar. Phoenixville. Aunt Matilda. Betrayal. Escape. Capture. Another Escape. Finchley. The Pit. The Tunnel. And now, the Nephrotic Syndrome.

After he finished, he sat and wiped tears from his eyes. He wasn't even crying, really. There was no sobbing or snuffling. His eyes were just watering.

The guy with the phone, for the first time since Brobson had begun speaking, moved. He let the phone drop and crabwalked towards Brobson.

"My name's Clifton," he told him. "You can call me Cliff. Or Bontz."

"Don't confuse him," Gale muttered.

Cliff waved this away. "What's your name, buddy?"

Ah. Brobson knew he'd forgotten a detail. "Brobson. Lutz. I don't have a nickname."

Cliff smiled.

"I'm Greta!" called the woman in front.

"Ian," the driver announced.

"Basil," declared the final bandmember. "Cliff, you should tell him about how *you're* gay!"

Exquisite toleration colored Cliff's smile. "Believe it or not, I was actually coming around to that."

Brobson marveled. A full-grown gay man! Living with straights! Not only that, but being cool! "You are? Really? Is it hard?"

Cliff shrugged. "Definitely not as hard as escaping crazies in the woods."

"*Seriously*," Basil affirmed.

Ian brightened up from the driver's seat. "Hey, Brobson, could we do a concept album about you? Like a musical story."

"The Quest for Phoenixville," Greta volunteered.

Ian bounced. "To The Kingdom of the Phoenix!"

"Rise of the Phoenix King!"

"GUYS," Gale snapped. He turned back to Brobson. "Here's the problem. You need to go to a hospital. You're in bad shape."

Brobson shook his head. "They'll call my parents. I can…if I just drink something, I'll be fine."

Gale and Clifton exchanged a glance. The latter asked Brobson, "are you aware that you've been slipping in and out of consciousness as we've been talking?"

Oh. He was not aware.

"What's your Aunt Matilda's last name?"

"I…I don't know." Brobson didn't think that was a fair question – what kid knows their Aunt's last name?

Another glance. Gale tried a new approach: "Do you know if she's related to your Dad or your Mom?"

"My…my Dad, I think."

"Is she married? Or has she ever been married?"

"I don't think so. I'm not sure."

Gale nodded, patted Brobson gently on the shoulder and turned to Cliff. "Her name might be Lutz, then. It's L-U-T-S?"

"L-U-T-Z."

Cliff nodded. "L-U-T-Z, Gotcha." He started doing something else with his phone. It wasn't a call.

"I got it," Basil announced.

Cliff put his phone away. "You get signal out here?"

"I get signal basically everywhere."

"Who's your carrier?"

Basil shrugged. "Dunno. My mom pays for my phone bill."

Gale continued his debrief. "You think she'd be understanding about the situation?"

"Sure," Basil replied. "Data charges are the s-"

"I was asking Brobson about his Aunt."

"Oh. Well, it's gonna be a bit of a drive for her to get here," Basil told his phone. "Looks like Phoenixville is three hours away."

"She'll come," Brobson maintained. He knew she would.

"Ok," Gale said. "Well, in that case, I vote we go to the hospital. We'll think of something to tell them about what happened. We'll tell them Ian's your brother."

"Why me?" Ian whined.

"Because you look most like him."

"How's that?"

"Dashingly handsome. Focus on driving."

Brobson was astonished: one straight guy calling another straight guy handsome. And nobody tried to fight anybody, or call each other hurtful names! What a strange, wonderful world.

"Greta's mom is a lawyer," he resumed. "She can try to help us figure out custody stuff, probably."

"Yeah!" Ian shouted. "We'll call child services!"

"What's…" Brobson couldn't be sure if he'd had a brain fart or passed out. Or maybe he'd had a little seizure like Uncle Pat. Or maybe he'd talked to whomever it was Keith Malamar checked in with mid-sermon. "Ah…custody?" He'd heard the word…

"Who you live with," Clifton explained. "You might be able to stay with your Aunt Matilda."

Brobson felt a hundred pounds lighter at the prospect. "For how long?"

Gale beamed at Brobson's evident relief. "Maybe forever."

It wasn't laughter, but Brobson definitely made some happy noises.

"Just seems worth noting," Greta amended, "that my mom does entertainment law."

Basil, still talking down to his phone, said "she must know custody lawyers though, right?"

Greta shrugged. "I guess? But I d-"

"Ah! Here." Basil handed his phone to Clifton.

Clifton's eyes tore across the screen. He nodded, a giant smile spreading across his face. There was more than enough smile for him to share with Brobson. "Does Aunt Matilda sell houses?"

"Yeah!" Brobson enthused. "That's her! She's an *aunt-er-pin-uer.*"

"She sure is," Cliff confirmed.

Gale looked a question at him.

"She won a community outreach award. They wrote it up in the paper, along with the name of her firm."

Cliff tapped the phone and few more times, then put it to his ear.

Greta turned around in her seat again. "Rise of the Phoenix King is really good, though."

Ian shook his head. "Too on the nose."

"I didn't *pick* Phoenixville."

"You picked 'rise'," Basil noted.

"What would you do, then?"

Basil pondered this, as Brobson felt himself lulled by the tiny ringing sound coming from Cliff's phone.

"Something about a Crown of Fire," he finally concluded. "It's a pretty badass image. That's an album cover, you know?"

"Maybe you should ask Brobson," Gale suggested.

Brobson could barely hear over the impossibly distant ringing in Cliff's ear. "Hm?"

"About using you as a concept."

"For an album," Ian added.

"You don't have to answer now," Greta was slow to clarify. "We're not vultures. It's just pretty…" she glanced at Ian, "…*brutal*, what you went through."

"Seriously," Basil once again affirmed. "I know guys twice your size who aren't half the man you are."

If that was meant to be flattery, it absolutely worked. Brobson feared he might never be able to stop smiling. It was the only fear worth having.

"I think that'd be pretty cool," Brobson finally said.

"Hiiii," Cliff said to his phone. "I'm calling from… TNS Equity, um, I was hoping I might speak with Ms. Lutz?"

Gale scooted over to the front seat, and asked Greta which hospital they were going to. In response, she pointed out the windshield.

"Ah," Gale said as he scooted right back to Brobson. "Remember, Ian's your brother. If they ask. And you..." Gale fumbled for an idea just out of reach. "How could this have happened?" he sourced to the rest of the band.

They all shrugged.

"We can't bring a kid this banged up to the hospital, while we're dressed like *this*, and not have an explanation!"

"Hi!" Cliff exclaimed. "Ms. Lutz? Hello!"

"We'll just have to wing it," Basil offered.

Cliff stuffed a finger in his ear as he continued his call "...Brobson, and something's..."

Greta spun all the way around now. "Just, if they ask you what happened, pretend you can't remember!"

Gale sighed. "Alright. I guess that's the plan."

"Ian's my brother," Brobson repeated, "and I don't remember what happened."

"Just until we can get figure out the next step."

"Ok."

"In the meantime," Cliff grinned, "we can tell them his Mom's on her way." He handed the phone to Brobson.

He took it with a trembling hand, and levered it delicately to his ear.

"Hello?"

"Brobson!" cried Aunt Matilda. "Oh my...I'm so

sorry!"

He'd never heard that word fall from a grown-up's lips, intended for his ears. At least, not in a way he'd believed. It was hard to grab hold of.

"It's not your fault," was all he could think to say in reply. Still, it was nice to hear it from somebody. Anybody.

The van screeched to a halt. Gale shouldered open the rear doors.

"I think I gotta go now," Brobson told her. "I'm at the hospital." Gale was already sprinting through the automatic doors, shouting about getting some help.

"I'll be there by the end of the day," Aunt Matilda assured him. "Oh, Brobson." That seemed to be a complete, independent thought.

In full battle regalia, Gale led a trio of utterly flummoxed-looking nurses down towards the van. Brobson watched them, more amused than anything. "Hey, Aunt Matilda?"

"What is it?" He could hear a great deal of movement on her end of the phone. The woman was hustling.

"I want Fischer to be my Valentine and that's just the way it is." He announced this much the same way he would a report card composed entirely of A's.

At this point, the nurses fell upon him with twelve-syllable words punctuated by six letter acronyms. They took the phone and handed it back to Cliff. Brobson only had time to thank his Aunt. He didn't hear what she had to say about his revelation.

Funnily enough, he didn't really care.

BUT THEY SAY *on moonless nights, deep in the thicket whence every howling wind that ever frightened a child draws breath, where even those spirits which roam the wildwood tread not for fear of what they might find...they say that even to this day, you can hear the crack of bats on bags, of belts on backs.*

And they say that, if you're not careful, you might find your way to a lonely booth...just like that one. And you might meet a man...quite like him. And he will say to you...

"Blessing!"

Even to this day.

Also by Jud Widing

Novels
A Middling Sort
Westmore and More!
The Year of Uh

Stories
Identical Pigs

Made in the USA
Middletown, DE
23 April 2021

38146490R00177